LONG LIVE SANDAWARA

Mudrooroo

ETT IMPRINT
Exile Bay

This edition published by ETT Imprint, Exile Bay 2020

First published by Quartet Books in 1979.
First paperback edition published by Hyland House in 1987.
Reprinted 1992.

ETT IMPRINT
PO Box R1906
Royal Exchange NSW 1225
Australia

Copyright © Estate of Mudrooroo 2019

ISBN 978-1-922473-24-0 (paper)
ISBN 978-1-925706-41-3 (ebook)

Cover painting: William Strutt, *Black Thursday* (detail).
Cover design by Tom Thompson.

LONG LIVE SANDAWARA

Every revolution needs a leader and there is no question in Alan's mind that he is that leader. For inspiration he goes to Noorak, the law holder of his people, and hears the heroic tales of Sandawara, the last of the warriors, who died defending his land and his people against the white man in the Kimberleys. So Alan names himself and becomes the new Sandawara and the rest of the unemployed teenage Aborigines of his mob take the names of Sandawara's followers. In his crash pad, a broken-down old house, the new Sandawara plots and schemes the revolution.

The story of this mob of anti-heroes, of a farcical inefficient revolution, gives a vivid portrayal of the new and frightening world of rootless youth, who lack identity and purpose and shoot as easily as they love because neither act has meaning.

CONTENTS

ONE

AT THE PUB

A heavy white cop fist had smashed Tom in the jaw for dumb insolence; but that was yesterday and today his dole cheque has arrived to ease the pain. He sits at the bar, finishes a beer and orders another from a scowling barmaid. Beside him sits a thick-set girl, quite light-skinned, but with the beetling brows, heavy cheeks and big-breasted body of the lubra. She's a friend of Tom's, but not a girl friend, though he would like her to be that for at least a night. His hand comes to rest on her thigh. She doesn't notice. Her attention is fixed on the man who has just slunk through the swinging doors.

Hat pulled low, eyes hidden behind mirror sunglasses; trench-coat belted tightly about his body, though it's a hot evening, the man stops just inside to give the bar a complete examination before committing himself. His hidden eyes stop and start from man to man sitting around the horseshoe shaped bar. Finally, he makes a decision and snakes his way toward the back of the room where Tom and the girl are sitting. Without speaking to them, he points for a beer and tosses it down with an exaggerated flip. Then he takes out the makings and slowly and carefully performs the rolling of a cigarette. At last he tosses it into the air and catches it in his lips. He pulls out a lighter, borrowed from Tom and never returned, thumbs flame on to the cigarette end and draws in, as if the smoke is marijuana. Two long draws diminish the cigarette to a butt. This he slowly stubs out in an ashtray, as if he's grinding it on the face of some enemy.

The girl is too conscious of the man sitting beside her and of his deliberate gestures. Her eyes still hold on to the ashtray as he gets to his feet. In a small mirror, reflecting from behind a row of bottles, she watches him adjusting his long coat, then pulling his hat brim down to touch the top of his sunglasses. His last action is to take out a newspaper and place it beside Tom, then he vanishes as if he has never been in the girl's view.

'He's creepy that one is,' the girl shudders, suddenly becoming aware of Tom's clutching hand and jerking it off with a tensing of muscle.

'Come on Sue, that's only Ron.' Tom replies, leaning over the bar top, gaunt as a sickly gum tree. 'He's nutty as a fruitcake, but harmless.'

He picks up the paper and stares at the front page.

'Well, what do you know, Alan's made the headlines, the little punk.'

Sue looks down and reads: 'Louts Disrupt Political Rally.'

'Oh that,' she exclaims, 'all he did was throw some crackers. I was there collecting signatures for the Aboriginal Land Rights petition.'

'Yeah,' Tom mutters, then begins reading aloud: 'Police arrested a youth, believed to be an Aboriginal, who allegedly created the disturbance and flung a weapon, a boomerang, at the speaker. It seems the boomerang was of the non-returning variety as is the honourable member of parliament who was addressing the gathering.'

'What'll happen to him?' the girl asks, deep voiced with concern.

'Arrh, you know our Alan,' Tom laughs. 'He'll be weeping, saying he's sorry and denying everything all in one breath. He's a cunning little snake and can con a rabbit out of its burrow.'

'Come on,' the girl says sharply. 'What, are you jealous or something? At least he always looks smart.'

'Well, I don't go around getting arrested for kiddy tricks.'

'No, only for drunkenness. He tries to help his people, not like you.'

'You call that helping his people?' Tom replies with a laugh. 'Hell, it's only stupid games and commy games at that. That red bastard, what's his name, who runs the East Wind Bookshop, has got him all mixed up. Should be a law against types like that.'

'Mr Miller was a good friend of ours. Anyway he's gone east now. It was Alan's idea to get a few boys together and demonstrate at the meeting.'

'Yeah, yeah,' Tom chants, then begins coughing, his face turning a sickly yellow. Sue, instinctively, puts a hand of comfort on his shoulder. The man recovers and manages a tremulous grin. 'Forget Alan, he'll be all right,' he says. 'He's only a kid, sixteen, and too young to go up on a charge. They'll let him go, just another drunken boong.'

Sue sees the bitter look on his face. 'Tom,' she says softly, 'when are you going to get a grip on yourself? You know you can't keep on like this. Why don't you smarten yourself up and find a job? It'll be for the best.'

'Why should I?' Tom mutters, becoming defensive. He stares down at his grubby jeans and army disposal shirt. Automatically he begins brushing his clothing, feeling the throbbing ache of his bruised cheek. Then his thin brown hand, slightly trembling, falls away like a bird unable to fly.

'Why should I?' he declares not only to Sue, but to the whole world. 'I'm happy as I am. I get by all right. Get enough to eat, to drink, got a place to doss down in. I'm happy enough. Can't think of anything else I want. Perhaps, maybe just to come into a bar like this and feel one of the boys. You know, just come in and feel welcomed. Arrh, who the hell cares?' he turns angrily on Sue. 'I'm all right, Jack, fuck you. I've got everything I need.'

'But you should care, Tom,' Sue tells him. 'You should care about yourself and about us. Don't just waste your life.'

'Conversation's too serious for me,' he replies, wanting to escape into numbness. Tom looks around and says with a sigh of relief: 'Anyway, here comes your boyfriend. I'll leave you two alone and get back to the pad.'

Tom hurries out into the soft evening air glad to get away from the girl. What answers has he got for his life? He stands outside the pub wondering where to go. A soft voice says 'hello' and he finds Gary standing beside him. Gary's a middle-class Anglo-Indian youth running away from his strict dad. He has told Tom that he wants to lead his own life which means forming a rock band and making a lot of money. Tom has heard too much of his guitar playing and considers it hopeless. At least the youth has got the crashpad together and lets them stay there, even though Alan and the others have just about taken it over.

They walk off together, Tom asking him where he has been.

'Practising,' the youth replies, his large open face wrinkled in thought. His big body lurches along. Good-natured at the best of times, he's not easy to upset, but the things moving in his pad seem to be getting heavy-and heavier.

'You know that Alan?' he says. 'He's a good kid, but kind of weird. Look what he did today.'

'Yeah,' Tom mutters.

'And the other day he brought this two foot long machete into the pad. Man, I'm for peace and love. I want to get my band together without hassles and play beautiful music.'

Disapproval is all over his face and Tom must pacify him. 'Well, you know, mate, pretty soon we're off roo shooting. The machete's to skin the buggers. Now all we need is a couple of rifles and we're in business. Man, look at the price of roo skins. We were all talking about it the other day. You want money for your band equipment; I want money to go back east, and going after roos is a good way to get it.'

He smiles into Gary's scowling face and watches it relax in agreement. Now, Tom feels, is the time to bring up another delicate subject. 'Your car's just rotting away in that vacant lot at the back of the pad,' he tentatively begins. 'It's a waste of a good set of wheels. Today Greg picked up a new battery and I tried to start it. No dice; but Greg, he knows a lot about engines and is going to get to work on it tomorrow. If the roo shooting does get off the ground we'll need transport.'

Tom glances at the youth's face as they pass a shop window and sees the forehead wrinkle. 'But Tom,' Gary protests, 'my licence is suspended. You know that time I almost ran that cop down? Lucky he thought it was an accident.'

'You and your peace and love,' Tom can't help saying with a grin. 'Anyway my licence is O.K. and we can use it – all of us.'

'But it's my car,' Gary protests.

'Come on, just trust us. Nothing'll happen to it. After all we are going to fix it for you. Just think how much that'd cost if you took it along to a garage.'

'Yeah, that's right, and today I lost my job selling those copper things.'

'Guess you'll be on the dole with the rest of us.'

'And it takes three weeks to get.'

'No worries, mate,' Tom smiles. 'We'll dob in more for the rent and pretty soon we'll be out after the roos.'

'That'll be fine. I saw this guitar I liked, but it costs a lot of bread.'

'No worries mate, no worries, you'll have it sooner than you think,' Tom exclaims playing on the youth's needs and wants. 'And Alan's got some good ideas on getting heaps of dough. One way or the other we'll make out.'

Gary's face relaxes and he smiles. 'Hope Rob's cooked up something better than those crepes suzettes he choked us with last night.'

They turn down the side street leading to the pad and walk under trees.

II

Rob has never tried his hand at *bullabesa* before and is anxiously waiting to see how it will turn out. Bumbling around the small kitchen he hasn't time for his full-bodied, dark-skinned girl friend, Rita, who brushes constantly against him. She is nervous about her first job and the youth sympathises with her; but he wishes she wouldn't get in his way. There's a time and place for everything, and right now in this kitchen, it is food. He chops three cloves of garlic, then lights the gas under the saucepan. Rita comes to peer over his shoulder as the oil bubbles. He adds vegetables, cleans a conger eel, shells some fresh mussels and shrimps. Cutting the seafood into pieces, not too small, he adds them to the vegetables. Rita presses against his spine, distracting him. He feels her breasts flattening against his back. But he hasn't time for that, not even when she reaches around and grabs at him.

'God, you're skinny,' the girl exclaims, running her hand along his ribs.

'At least you're a handful,' Rob answers absently, his thin brown face puckered in concentration. How will the soup turn out? He's made a mistake, the shellfish should have been added later. He turns the gas low. It's almost time to add the water. The youth fusses around the kitchen, exasperating the girl. She undoes his pants and slips her hand in. Adding the water, Rob tries to ignore his hard on. He lets the whole concoction simmer, checks the time, then sits at the table which is against the wall opposite the stove and sink. He jumps up. He has forgotten to add salt and pepper and a pinch of saffron. Rita grimaces in disgust. She follows him to the stove and back to the table. Now, the youth has to slice some bread and fry it. He reaches for the bread, then stops with a gasp. Rita has crawled under the table and, pretending to be some ferocious animal, sinks her teeth into his ankle.

III

The pad has only three rooms. A small passage leads to a large bedsitting room to the left and to the kitchen on the right. Straight ahead is the bathroom. Near the kitchen a door leads from the passage to a narrow yard which is surrounded by a high sheet iron fence. In the large room, Greg does pushups and is past the two hundred mark. Every time he raises his body from the floor his grey eyes reach a painting of a black man holding a rifle like a spear, his body held in tension and his head turned, as if trying to catch a glimpse of pursuers. This is Sandawara, a black freedom fighter who began the struggle too late. If Greg turns his head slightly he can see a badly lettered sign: ANARCHY FOR THE NEXT WHITE YEARS. He doesn't know what it means, nor does he care. His thoughts are on Rita and Rob in the kitchen. Desperately, jealously, he wants to know what they are doing. He wants Rita, but she has eyes only for the skinny bloke. He can't see what she finds in him. His body is better, he can knock out a sheep with one blow and he knows he's a handsome hunk of manhood – still Rita hardly deigns to notice him. He gets to his feet, fed up with the pushups and flexes his muscles. In tiptop condition, but what does it get him? Sweet fuckall! The youth begins shadow boxing, admiring himself in a mirror. Perhaps he should go out and pick a blue with someone. He hears the scraping of the bike being wheeled out, then the slam of the side door followed by the tinny clang of the gate being flung open. A silence as the bike is pushed through, then the clang of the gate.

He stands listening until all sound is lost. He decides he wants a cup of coffee. Greg swaggers down the passageway and into the kitchen where the runt's tasting his cooking. Rob looks up.

'Have some soup, it's good, a Spanish thing called *bullabesa*,' the cook smiles at Greg while pouring him a bowlful.

Greg takes the soup. If it wasn't for Rita, he would take Rob for some sort of queer. Why, he could break him in half without raising a sweat. His grey eyes turn blank as he contemplates the breaking, but it'd completely ruin his chances with the girl as well as getting him tossed out of the pad.

'It's a little woppish,' he judges, spooning the liquid down, liking and not liking it. 'What'd you put in it?' he demands.

'Lots of stuff, it's the garlic that makes it Italian-like,' the cook replies, watching anxiously to see if Greg really likes the soup. At least, Muscle-head's getting it down, taking great slurping gulps. Rob feels relieved. Yesterday no one ate his concoction.

'The others should've been here by now,' Rob says. 'They better get here fast if they want it hot.'

'Where'd Rita go?' Greg asks, his jealousy rising up. To spite the cook he adds ketchup and feels good when Rob winces.

'Out to get some groceries from that selfservice store down the road.'

'Could've gone along to give her a hand,' Greg mutters, finding that ketchup doesn't go with *bullabesa*. He finds something rubbery in his mouth and spits it out.

'Only a mussel,' Rob explains, then adds, 'Rita wanted to do the shopping on her lonesome. A sort of test, see!'

'Yeah,' Muscles grunts. No chick of his would've been allowed to break into a shop by herself. He feels more contempt for Rob, but stifles it. One day Rita would turn his way. It is as sure as the stars in heaven.

The side gate clangs, followed by the slamming of the door. Both look into the passageway.

'Only Charly,' Greg says, finishing off the bowl and holding it out for a refill. The soup is delicious.

In the living room a guitar starts to plonk out a hillbilly, four chord strum and a rough voice begins:

They needed a new star in heaven
And they couldn't find a brighter one to shine;
And though she was only seven,
They took her off to heaven,
That little kid sister of mine.

Both wince at the song. Charly's like that, especially after a bottle or two. A country boy, he likes sentimental songs.

'Fuck,' Greg says, loud enough to be heard in the other room.

Charly plonks out the last chord sequence with his big hard hand, then flings the guitar on to the four mattresses spread across the floor along one wall of the room. He runs his fingers through his thick matted hair, hitches up his ex-army pants, buttons his denim jacket and leaves without a word to Gary and Tom as they brush past him. Tom thinks he detects a nod of greeting from the lost youth, but it's hard to tell with Charly who's either very dumb or wandering in some distant world where the rivers flow with cheap plonk.

Gary, his mind on his music, picks up the guitar, strums it, finds it tuned and begins a raunchy number from the top forty. Instantly, Greg, the drummer in the projected band, runs in and picks up his drumsticks. He pounds away on the top of the coffee table. Tom, feeling more than a little dizzy, falls on to the mattresses, but rises on one elbow to take the bowl of soup Rob brings him. He takes a slurp and fin.ds it garlicky. Hungry, he drains the bowl. The band falls to a halt as Gary gets soup and Greg coffee.

'Almost got the group together,' the future bandleader informs his future drummer. 'You better pick up a set of drums soon so we can have some real practice. Got to get a lot of songs together, too. How'd you like the Flaming Dicks as the band name?'

'How'd you like Charles Atlas?' Greg replies, giving a rap on the table which finally collapses into a heap of firewood.

'No, not classy enough.'

'Maybe, maybe,' Muscles replies, annoyed that his name's been so lightly dismissed.

'Why not Jealousy?' Tom breaks in, putting the soup bowl on the floor. Knowing that Greg has the hots for Rita, just as he has them for Sue, he gets a certain pleasure in needling the youth. Greg, thick-headed as well as thick-bodied, rarely catches on. Irony completely escapes him.

'No, too mouldy,' he answers. 'No dash in it.' He turns to Gary. 'By the way, been working all afternoon on your car. Should run like a bomb now. With wheels we'll be ready for anything, even kidnapping the Governor's daughter.'

Gary flinches. All this talk of violence and crime is wearing him down. He doesn't like it one bit, and if it wasn't such a great pad, he'd get out. It started with that kid Alan, rapping about taking what's rightfully theirs – not his, but those Abos'. Then that Greg scares him. Why, he hasn't even heard him play on a set of drums and doesn't know how he sounds. When he gets his group together, he wants it to be really great and make money. He looks at the vicious Greg, the drunk Tom, and feels his plans threatened. Now they're taking over his car without a by your leave. God, he needs something to get his mind out of the dark clouds.

Something at the side gate scrapes through. It clangs shut; the door slams; and Rita bustles into the room hauling a huge bag of groceries. Gary takes one look, shakes his head and moans, 'God!'

'Wow, man, it was a cinch,' the girl yells out. 'Not a pig in sight. I got everything Rob wanted. More!' and she rushes around the room excitedly and stops before a poster of Ho Chi Minh. 'Old granddad always gives me luck.' She looks at Rob. 'Help me get this to the kitchen.'

They leave and Tom raises his eyebrows towards a scrawled sign, LABOUR FOR LABOUR. No one likes that particular political party, but

Alan believes such signs give them a cover – like the other signs, SLAM WHITLAM WITLESS and FRASER IS CRAZY. He looks from the signs to Muscles who's pacing about in jealousy. Greg knows what the two are doing in the kitchen. But, perhaps, not this time, for the girl returns after ten minutes followed by a not exhausted Rob. Tom smiles, remembering that the cook has confided that he has trouble keeping up with the horny girl.

She darts to the centre of the room, then after posing there a minute, fumbles in her jeans and tugs out a cloth bag. Then she scratches a breast, almost making Greg pant, and says: 'Got some grass, let's blow it.'

Tom sits up, he can always do with a blast. Rita comes to the mattresses and plonks herself down. She brushes the hair out of her eyes; looks through the rubbish scattered over the floor; finds a sheet of newspaper, and cleans the weed on it. The seeds are carefully placed in a matchbox. They have every intention of seeding half Perth.

Again the girl fumbles through the junk on the floor, to find a packet of cigarette papers and a filter butt. Sticking three of the papers together, she rolls the joint with the filter, lights it, takes a deep drag and passes it to the waiting Tom. Greg and Rob edge nearer for their share, and so does Gary after a brief struggle. He needs it.

'Good shit,' Tom lets out the words with a stream of smoke. 'Best I've had for a long time. Where'd you get it from?' He grabs the joint back from Gary.

'You know,' Rita mutters, reaching for the smoke. 'Rob and me were walking in the city the other day and this guy stopped and gave us a lift in his car. He took us to his flat, very posh, and he had about a pound of this stuff – even cocaine. But he wanted to get it off with both of us and we're not into that. He was a nice guy, didn't insist, and gave us the dope when we left.'

'Would've knocked his fucking head off,' the aggressive Greg says, 'and taken the lot.'

'Yeah, you would have,' Rita throws him a cold look which makes him hate her and think of rape. 'Yeah, you would have, and what about if he was a big crim type? What do you think'd happen to you? One has to stay cool, just as Alan says, till you know what you're up against.'

'Yeah, that's right,' Greg manages to agree. Alan's all right by him. He's where the action is or will be. He sees himself sitting before a brand new shiny set of drums.

The dope makes Rita horny and she begins to rub her boyfriend's thigh. Tom puts out the centre light and lights a candle. The girl takes advantage of the half light to brush Rob's prick till he has a hard on.

'What about you and me making some coffee, huh?' she says, and they're getting up when a loud crash comes from the kitchen, followed by the sound of glasses crashing from the windowsill. Instantly Rob is alarmed for his territory and his hardness softens.

A voice, rough and harsh, erupts from the kitchen. 'Bloody hell,' and they laugh as they realise it's Ron. They don't trust the nut and quickly put the joint out. Rita stuffs the rest of the dope back into her jeans as the man enters the room. His mirrored sunglasses reflect their faces back down to them.

Gary's annoyed at the man for bursting in and shouts: 'Ron, why do you keep coming here? You know you're not welcome. And why do you come in through the window? How many glasses have you broken this time? You know the door's always unlocked. Man, why the hell do you do these things?'

Ron ignores Gary and leers at Rita. Then, with a certain flair, he raises the great snout of his nose to snuff up the air. 'Funny smell in here. How about some coffee?'

Rob, always eager to feed people if the cooking is his own, immediately agrees, much to Gary's annoyance. 'There's still some soup on the stove. You're welcome to it.'

'Thanks mate, you're not like some I could name,' the man grates out and sidles out of the room, or rather begins a sidle and vanishes – to appear with a bowl of soup. 'Dago grub,' he growls, downing the bowl and disappearing for another.

Gary yells: 'Just remember you don't pay for the tucker here.'

'So what?' Ron voices, seeming to materialise in the middle of the room, this time without the bowl. He's drained the pot in the kitchen. The man prowls around.

'What's with these?' he queries, putting his face in front of one of the crudely lettered slogans. 'Nice painting,' he gestures elaborately at the picture of Sandawara. 'We did painting in the asylum. What nut did this one?'

'Rebel Hooper,' Tom mutters, staring at himself in the sunglasses and not liking it. He looks at Rita's breasts for relief. Sometimes, he thinks, they are there for his touching, but mates don't do the dirty on one another. 'He's in jail. Beat up some white bloke who sold him a bottle of watered wine.' He smiles as Ron flinches. The man bragged about doing the same thing, with about the same result – the Nungar didn't take it lying down, but robbed Ron of what money he had on him.

'Anyway,' Gary begins, 'why'd you come here, Ron? Just why do you come here?'

'Now don't start on me, will you? You know I've been in a mental hospital for seventeen years. Alan told me to come any time I want to. He wants to get the shit out of my head. He's helping me, not like you.'

Gary sees himself reflected in the mirror sunglasses. 'Well, has he got any of it out?'

Ron, a whine in his voice, 'You know he's trying. It's all right for you to talk. You're not even an Australian. There was a bloke like you in the mental hospital. One of you Indian fellows. He was a pig. Used to beat up the patients. I know what sort your sort is like, that I do.'

The Anglo-Indian stares and, put out by his reflection, looks at the floor. 'Ron, why are you so prejudiced? I heard what you've been saying about me in Obelia's. You hate everyone, don't you? Wogs and wops and spics and gooks.'

'Gary, I don't hate anyone – only people like you.'

Greg darts in. 'Ron, where's the forty cents you owe me? Two weeks, man, is two weeks too long. You said pension day!' Muscles cracks his knuckles and stares at the nut. The glasses don't put him off.

Ron shrugs and goes on the defensive. 'I came yesterday. Got my pension and came right over. You weren't here!'

Greg pounds his fist into his palm. 'That's a baldfaced lie. You didn't turn up yesterday. I was working on Gary's car at the back and would've seen you.' He scowls, 'Come on, hand it over!'

The man mutters inaudibly, before raising his voice: 'Didn't see you here. Came here, weren't no one here. Then after I went to see Janet. Been at her place all the time. Know what she did, that slut of a bitch? Borrowed fifty dollars off me, then had her boyfriend fling me out. Don't know why I go to see her? Guess it's love. Know when she has a shit, she leaves the door open? Even when she showers. But she won't let me touch her. All those sluts are like that, the whole flaming lot. One day I'll take a knife to her, that I will.'

Greg sighs in exasperation: 'Ron, every pension day, it's the same old story. You're a lunatic.'

Ron cackles: 'Well, it gets me ninety dollars a fortnight, more than you get on the dole.'

Tom, lying on the mattress, yawns and says, 'Ron, why do you hate women? All the time they're sluts and bitches. Yet, you're always sniffing around Janet. Why?'

The man senses some friendliness, or harmlessness in Tom and goes into a well rehearsed patter. 'Tom, I don't hate them. Look, I just gave Janet fifty dollars; is that hate? Anyway, they all do the dirty on me. Use me and throw me out. What do you expect; why shouldn't I hate them? I hate being used, taken advantage of.' Spittle edges to the corner of his mouth. The grey stubble of his beard catches a few drops. 'I spent seventeen years in the loony bin, seventeen fucking years; all because of a little slut, a lying bitch of twelve. She said I did this and that to her; I didn't!' He grins. 'Though I might have done it to my sister. She was thirteen and we lived in the country. No one liked me, even then, but she did, the hot little bitch. Sis, well she used to come out in the bushes and we played these games. We both liked them games; but that wasn't the reason they put me in the mad house. It was long after, and all because of a lying little slut. I never touched her. They're all like that. You know, I was at this cat house tonight and I gave this fat blonde, she had these great big tits (I like that), twenty dollars. You know what? – she wanted me to wash first. Refused to let me do it until I did. I told that slut off, and they flung me out into the street, just like that; I'm going back for my money. They're all like that, take everything and give you nothing ...'

Gary can't take any more and breaks in, 'You lunatic, you're sick, and your head's full of shit.'

Ron turns serious and calm. 'I know, Gary, I know.' He wipes the spittle from his chin. 'Don't think I don't know it. But Alan, he's a good kid, said he'll help me to get the shit out of my head. That's why I come here. He's not like you.'

The Anglo-Indian sneers: 'Don't you know he laughs at you? Anyway, the more shit he shovels out, the more you put back in. Fancy relying on a kid to help you. You're fifty if a day and yet you listen to a young kid. You're out of your mind.'

The man turns nasty: 'It's because of people like you that I'm where I am. I know what you wogs are like. There was this bloke in the loony bin. He was supposed to be looking after us and you know what he did? He bashed us every chance he got! You Indians are all alike. Soft and slimy on the outside, out for number one on the inside. And don't think they don't know what a bullshitter you are in Obelia's.' He looks around for allies. 'You ain't like Tom here or Greg or Rob. You never gave anyone a cent in your life.' He fumbles around in his pocket and manages to find a ten cent coin. 'Here Greg, I'll give you the other next time I see you. We're Aussies, not like him, we're mates and help each other. Lend me ten cents, I'll pay you back tomorrow,' and he pockets the coin before Greg can reach out and take it.

Gary loses his temper: 'Listen you, this is my pad, not Alan's, and I don't want you here. None of us want you here – get out!'

Ron looks around and finds no kindness. 'All right, I'm going. All right, I'm going, but one day I'll get you for this. At least when Alan's here, I can come. When he's around, you can't do nothing! Too scared to, ain't you? All you can do is pick on blokes like me who've been inside for seventeen years. Anyway I'm going, but I'll get all of you for this.'

Muscles gets to his feet; but Ron does his vanishing act and is nowhere in sight. One moment he's been in front of them, the next somewhere else. The door and gate don't slam, and Greg bounces out to check. Ron's been known to hide in the kitchen, waiting to reappear when they've cooled down.

The youth returns: 'He's gone, not a sign of him. How does he do it?' As he finishes speaking, there's a loud crash on the roof, followed by another and another. Ron is venting his anger by tossing bricks. 'I'll get him,' Muscles shouts, dashing from the room. Gary follows to see the fun, if any.

Tom grins: 'Five dollars to a cent, he doesn't. How about another J, Rita?'

The girl exclaims with a grin, 'After that, I need one."

'He's had a bad deal,' the man answers, looking at her.

'We all have,' Rita replies, pulling out her stash bag and beginning to roll the smoke. 'What about me? Mum doesn't even know who my dad is. She doesn't care a fuck about me either. I came across her on the street the other day, and she wouldn't even say "hello" to me, her own daughter. She's married to some straight guy now with a steady job and money in the bank. You know, she's made it. They've even put her in charge of a Nungar day care centre. Imagine that, looking after kids and her with no time for her own kid.'

Rob, in sympathy, begins to give the tearful girl a backrub. She cheers up and finishes rolling the joint. 'Let's get some coffee,' she says to her boyfriend, 'and then we'll smoke.'

The cook agrees. 'I better clean up the mess Ron made. He really wolfed down my soup, didn't he? Gee Rita, I want to check out the groceries. I'll make something special tomorrow, I mean today.'

They go into the kitchen, leaving Tom by himself. He finds a cigarette, lights it and puffs away, debating whether to go to the early opening pub or not. Muscles comes back from his fruitless search, sees that the couple are missing and begins to sulk. In spite he picks up the joint and lights it.

'Didn't find the old bugger,' he mutters. He passes the joint to Tom, then slams his fist into the palm of his hand. 'I'll get that bastard!'

'Arrh, forget about him,' Tom says, 'he's a loony. He can't help it.' He passes the smoke and reaches for the transistor radio. The heavy beat of the all night rock station hits out softly. Something's wrong with the speaker, the volume can't be adjusted and the sound's very distorted. But who cares? The dope fumes drift about the room.

The gate bangs, the door opens and slams and in rushes an excited Alan with two teenybopper Nungar girls in tow, light-skinned girls of about sixteen who, out of their element, stare around the dowdy room, not knowing what to do. Alan comes to a halt in the middle and stands there, his slim body taut. He grins from ear to ear. 'They couldn't keep a good man in,' the youth drawls, staring at the painting of Sandawara, 'just like they couldn't keep him down.'

'Don't say you broke jail,' Tom calls, 'and where did you find this jail bait?'

Alan looks across at him and sees the joint. 'Listen man, drugs are not part of our thing. Put it out!'

The man tries to outstare the youth, but his eyes slide away. Tension fills the room until the smouldering dope is doused. 'Sorry man, we don't see eye to eye on this.'

'Can't you see they want you to like it; want you to crave it – just like they want you on the grog?'

'Maybe, maybe,' Tom mutters, wishing for a drink, then he manages a grin. 'Anyway, where did they put you?'

Alan spins around. 'In a detention centre. I just walked right out of that place, along with these two. Meet Sally and Jane, two recruits. They don't know what to do with themselves, but I'll teach them things.' He grins at them and the two bewildered kids flash return smiles.

'Right on,' they say in unison.

'Let's crash for a few hours,' Alan calls. 'We'll get things together in the afternoon. It's just coming on to dawn.' He spins around, changing his mind with his motion. 'No, I've already slept an hour or two in that place. I'm off to see a friend, look after these two.'

With a grin, he races from the room, and Tom breathes a sigh of relief and relights the joint. The door slams and then the gate. 'It'll be the last one for sure,' the man says to no one in particular, then adds: 'Wonder if Alan is right about them turning us on to it?' He looks at the two standing girls. 'Sit down, or lie down if you want to sleep. Alan'll be back in a couple of hours.'

'He's some kid,' Sally murmurs to Jane as they stretch out on the mattresses.

TWO

DREAMS OF THE KIMBERLEYS

Noorak is the original Jacky Jacky. Shapeless and old, he lives under the railway bridge at Midlands. Thin and wizened, doddering with age, cold in ugly second hand clothing he's never grown used to, the old man crouches, dreaming, in front of a small fire. His mind drifts in warm wine thoughts about a time, not of his youth, but when he's less stiff – when his body's a pliant leather strap of authority above his people – until the white men, the policemen take him away south to an imprisonment far from his naked free land. Five years change him, load him with despair, dump him in the far south with a bottle of wine. The leather strap is stiff and hard, all pliability lost. To bend is pain. But before, he dreams; but before, his mind drifting above scenes of awful power; but before, he's Keeper of the Law, Bossman in his knowledge.

How powerful to be filled with the wisdom of the Law, and able to act within the Law – able to be that Law, until the day they take him away from his land, from his people, from the source of his power. He turns from Noorak to Jacky Jacky, imprisoned behind high walls. His sunken eyes, red with age and too much cheap wine, watch the few flickers of his fire.

Again, the old man sees himself standing strong. His hair caked with grey mud from the waterhole; his man scars, marked with white clay, taut like strands of rope across his back and chest. On either side of him other old men squat, copies of him. Behind them in terrible silence, the men of the tribe sit; behind him the youths, and further back the women and children. Together, bound and unified by the Law, they watch and wait for the Keeper to speak – wait in dread as no one will ever wait again. They have taken his power from him as they have taken his land. Again, the flames flicker; he feels the strands of red wool about his head; he feels the power flow through him. The Law is one, unchangeable – the protection of the people. The Law broken, they scatter, die and blow like dust before a wind. The Law says: 'Yabala must die.' The old men say: 'Yabala must die.' Yabala knows the Law says: 'Yabala must die.' It is right for him to die! The collective sigh, of terror, of awe, of relief echoes the verdict.

The old men gently take the outcast, the lawbreaker and lay him flat on his back. Noorak, no not Noorak, the Law itself takes up the soulstone and rubs it slowly between his palms, spits on it and rubs it again. The Law kneels down beside the young man, pauses, then passes the stone over Yabala's belly. Softly, the spirit is called out to enter into the man's body, so that when the night gives way to the sun, it will carry Yabala's soul to the dreaming country. Then all shall be well, the people shall endure, shall last; be strong and firm in oneness.

The fire flickers and the strands around his head grow heavier and heavier with the loss of his power. A band of iron fastens around his neck, a long chain drags him to the ground, pulling him away from his people to the deadland of the south – to the land of strangers, unknown and terrifying. His power goes, his skin slackens and wrinkles, his almost sightless eyes turn blood red with drink. His power goes, leaving only a trembling old body, soulless and almost alone.

Alan stands at a little distance from the fire. He stands lithe and straight as the spear which he has never held. He watches the old man while the sky lightens about him and a new day rises. Alan has never seen the old man lie down, nor has he seen the fire out. Dreaming dreams the youth cannot understand, the old man sits stooped over his tiny blaze while a new day glows in the sky. Alan, gently, with a tenderness he rarely shows before others, moves close to the old man and squats across from him, not even trying to keep the dust from his clothing. Without a word, he pushes across a bottle of sweet wine and some soft hamburger meat which the old fellow can chew with his toothless gums.

Noorak sighs, watching the last fading of the keeping of the Law. It has been broken, the people are scattered – would a wholeness ever return? Again, a memory flickers. The men take up their heavy stabbing spears. Power flows with his gesture. The spears descend to stab low at the thighs, are twisted and withdrawn. They stab higher and higher. It is the Law; but the policemen come and the Law is nothing in their eyes. The Lawkeeper becomes an outlaw, unable to defend his earth and his Law against aliens with a different law.

Slowly, he begins to speak; softly, he begins to speak – then more strongly. Alan bends forward, like a rifle, to catch every word. His large dark eyes cling tightly to the withered lips.

'The Law is good; the Law is the people; the Law is the land. Broken, the people are broken. Grass seeds, they scatter on the wind, take root, perhaps grow, but they are no longer the people.'

Noorak's shaking hand, like the claw of an eagle, reaches out, clutches a piece of meat and raises it to his mouth. The youth watches the gums chew, watches the claw clasp the bottle and lift it to withered lips.

'One drop of water by itself is nothing.' The rustling of the words are leaves under a dust laden breeze. 'It disappears into the ground without effect, but many drops make a torrent which sweeps away everything in its path. Water clings together. What makes it cling together is the Law. Without it, there are only isolated drops. Our Law is gone and I, the Keeper of the Law, let it go. Shall I ever find it and pass it on before I die; can I make it grow even a little when I have no land and no people? I am old, soon I shall die. Still I dream, dream of the time when the Law is strong and dream of passing it on with the sacred things which lie hidden in my lost earth. There, now it's just after the rains, the grass stalks wave in the breeze and the people are heavy and lazy with food.'

The old man falls silent and raises his bottle. Falling into dreams, once again as a child, he sits with the women away from the men beyond the firelight. Breathless he watches, caught in the web of the Law reaching far beyond him past the borders of the earth. The ancient songs flow into him, the click of the sticks move with the beat of his heart. Spurts of dust rise as dancers mime the everyday of life, moving in a oneness of creation reaching beyond the beginning and end. The kangaroo leaps and dies in mime; the serpent writhes and twists in seeming death to give them life. He sighs as the vision leaves. His voice rises to the sun to declare: 'I will return to die where I was born.'

The youth, filled with an emotion he cannot understand, listens to the words describing a life he has never known. He thinks of the white man who has spoken to him of a world where everyone is a loving brother or sister. He longs for that state. A vast loneliness sweeps over him-which he does not understand or care to understand. Then, he grins. In youth, ideals can still become a reality. He can fight to regain a wholeness. With a rush, Alan tosses off the deep mood that age has plunged him into and says: 'Granddad, tell me of Sandawara, the great fighter, tell me about him.'

Noorak drinks more wine, pokes at the fire and lets his mind drop into visions that flow from him in words.

'Before, the strangers are few; we, many! Then, it becomes we that are the few. Even in Sandawara's time, the Law is passing, even then it appears too late; but he is a man, a warrior who wants to fight them who are taking our earth and destroying us. At first he works with them. At first, he is taken in by their guile. They work on his greed, on his ambition, and his own people are to him as dust. For years he follows the white fellows, follows them against his own brothers. He treads them as the dust, as the dust that the white men's boots kick up into his face. He, a leader, is blind. He, as fleet as a goanna, follows, stumbling behind the heavy boots marching his people into captivity. A few, then many rise, but one by one they are taken and chained, chained like dogs and led away like dogs on a leash. The white fellows sing him with a false name: Eaglehawk. And he helps and by helping is bound as his people are. He cannot fly; white ashes cover the burning coals beneath. They smoulder until one day they're fanned into flame by the warrior, Ellewara. He, too, goes out against the white men; he, too, goes out to free his land, but for all his bravery, for all his cunning – and he is cunning – he is not a Sandawara, is not the leader. He is only the one who comes before, the one who shows the way, the way which might lead to death, but a warrior's death – a man's death!'

The old man's words rustle forth like dead leaves. His words rise and fall, reach out and trap the boy's ears. Alan listens to the tales of long ago, when men were men and went out to do and, finally, to die.

II

Eaglehawk and Captain, both trackers against their own people, are out after the so-called outlaw, Ellewara. Naked, except for belts holding revolvers and handcuffs, trusted because considered tame, the two move in silent motion across the darkened plain towards the soak where their quarry is known to be, his whereabouts betrayed by his boasts and the husband of Wandara, his woman.

Straight and tall, like the spears they have long discarded for the gun, deep chested, long sinewy legs built for endurance, for speed, fiery eyed and intelligent, they move confidently amid the terrors of the night. They know they will get their man. Effortlessly the two, with long loping strides, glide across the plain; effortlessly they twist through shadowy timber stands without fear; move over a creek without a splash or lap of water on banks to give them away, to alert their quarry, almost as deadly as they are; but they will get him!

Dawn breaks as they reach the edge of the densely tangled scrub which surrounds the waterhole. The edge is an almost solid wall, a seemingly dark impenetrable wall of closely growing small trees laced with vines; but only the depth of the waning night gives the imagined solidity. They worm their way onwards through the tangled scrub. Touch means all. Eaglehawk writhes his way onwards, followed by his mate, Captain. Vines and leafy branches brush their bodies, silently. Their dark and supple bodies twist and thrust onwards through the dense and matted undergrowth – silently! Not a twig snaps, not a vine rustles. Soundlessly feet press down and move onwards; forwards to the prey, dangerous and every bit as bushwise as they are. Every bit – but he cannot hear what cannot be heard; he cannot see what are only shadows, quiverings of tree boughs, swayings of vines.

In the grey dawn the manhunters stop and peer out into the little clearing of grass at the very heart of the scrub. Is Ellewara, he who has come out against all white men, there? A coiled black patch, the calmly sleeping body of Ellewara, the warrior; and next to him, a smaller patch, lies his woman, Wandara, safe against his side. Beside her rest the man's two hunting dogs, asleep and unaware.

In the fast growing light, Eaglehawk's eyes seek for the outlaw's weapons. Their quarry sleeps, his head pillowed on his left arm. Beside his right hand, ready to be snatched up, lie his spears. Eaglehawk takes the handcuffs from his belt without a clink of metal on metal, or even of metal against skin. He glides forward. Beside him cat-foots Captain with a cocked revolver. A harsh click, click and Ellewara is caught. The captive awakens, slowly and uncomprehendingly, wonderingly, then with a rush of understanding. His mouth gapes, then relaxes in a savage grin. His dogs slink away, his woman leaps up like a startled wallaby, takes in the scene in one horrified glance, and is away into the scrub. The man-hunters let her go. They have their prey.

'You've got me,' Ellewara says, he who has boasted that he will never be run to earth. Is it the bravado of the warrior which causes him to take his capture so lightly, or is there something else? For Ellewara has the power to sway men. Now he chuckles. His black bearded, rugged face splits with a surprising good humour which causes the others to grin in return. Already, the three men can feel the bonds of a certain comradeship.

'I have you,' Eaglehawk replies, losing his grin and scowling. He feels that he is the captive, not the proud man before him.

To show his freedom, his authority, he picks up the warrior's spears, balancing each at the throw, testing them for their feel. He knows a good weapon, and these spears are like the right hand of Ellewara. One by one, Eaglehawk puts his foot on each war spear and the sudden snap is hard and harsh, like the breaking of an arm. The useless sticks lie on the ground.

It's been the right thing for a police boy to do and Ellewara looks on grimly. 'A pity,' he grunts, 'they were good spears.'

In silence, the three men look down at the broken shafts. They turn away with regret. It is a cool sunny morning, a good time for hunting, for their kind of hunting – for food. They emerge on to the plain and begin the twenty mile trek back to captivity.

The blazing sun springs higher to turn the land red. On the wide eroded plain the small group seems lost. Naked and alone, each in himself, they fall into isolated thoughts. Only the rattle of speech from the garrulous Ellewara bridges the space between each man, summoning from the cool inner depths a common fire of thought. Each knows his land is being raped; each knows, two have been separated and tamed, but the words of the free one pass, trying to raise their temperature to that of the earth.

Ellewara's deepset eyes sparkle from face to face. He talks to friends. This man has travelled from the Oscar Range to the Lennard River, from the Barrier to the King Leopold Ranges – he treats each tribal territory as his own and is at home everywhere except in the white man's prison. And everywhere he goes his words ring out, drawing a response and a sympathy. Men see in him a somewhat rash brother and are drawn to him. He travels hostile country without bothering to hide his tracks. Now his voice rings out over the plain with a sobriety which fans the fire within.

'It's a pity,' he declares, 'that the riverbank people have fallen prey to the white skins and that the flat country men have gone the same way. You know what the white man calls you – tamed! Are we animals, are we like his stupid fat cows? No!' His savage shout bounds across the dry red earth like a warcry. 'They get nothing from whity, but work. They slave like women to help him take our earth. He's taken the big waterholes with the sweet grassy flats; he's chopped down our sacred trees to pollute our holy dance grounds with his ugly houses. He takes the water and grass. He drives away the kangaroos and wallabies; he murders the ducks and geese, and poisons even the very fish in our rivers. He kills everything, not for food, but through bloodlust. He leaves us nothing, not even our women – and what do we do? Slave and suffer, not for ourselves, but for him! Our kangaroos and emus, even our lizards and snakes are going; our birds – even our blood. He drives us into the deserts and barren hills to die, while he enslaves the weak ones to do his dirty work. This is true. It is! Lies flow from his tongue, not from mine. It is true, isn't it?'

He stops talking to let them think. They walk on. On the hot air the sun floats to noon. They walk on and think, Eaglehawk and Captain. Their faces become as harsh as the frowning hills rising in rocky desolation above the plain: their plain, their hills! Ellewara, he who can sway men, glances from one to the other, and his voice grates out: 'Gutless people, they've given the very earth to the aliens. And it is not theirs to give. It is the land of our ancestors and our children. And worst of all, without us, the white man would die. Without us, he would be powerless and could do nothing. You and you and others like you help our enemies, help them to destroy us. It's well that the police use us against ourselves. Oh yes, it's well!'

'Why?' snarls Eaglehawk, the tracker happy with his revolver at his waist and the power of the white man in his hands. 'And why?' he shouts out, his hand clasping his power.

'And why?' the astute Ellewara smiles. 'And why? Without us, without you he could never find us, could never catch us, could never walk across our earth and keep his life. That is why!' He laughs without mirth. His fiery eyes flame from one captor to the other, meeting frowns and wordless lips.

They stride on with their prisoner, but they are trackers, they work for the police for sugar, flour and tea: how can they even think revolt?

'But we're trackers ...' Eaglehawk suddenly jerks out, his eyes going to Captain for affirmation. 'We're trackers, we ride with the police ...' to be stopped with a hiss from Ellewara: 'Aren't you going to join us?'

'Join us?' Eaglehawk stumbles over the words. 'Join you,' he repeats, his feelings flowing across the plain to the distant wrecked hills eroded into mere stumps of rock. 'If I go with you, I'll be hunted; they'll hunt me,' he ends with a snarl of indecision.

'Shoot them!' Ellewara doesn't waste words – this time! He senses the power in the police boy, the awakening power.

The two trackers stare at one another, then turn eyes on their captive. 'Shoot them,' scoffs Eaglehawk, hiding the confusion in his heart, hiding thoughts and feelings he can't face: he would rather shoot Ellewara!

'Shoot them,' the warrior hisses again. The words slither towards them like serpents. Their thoughts are as hot as the sun.

'And where are we to get the guns to battle the police?' Eaglehawk asks scornfully to evade the command.

'You have your revolver,' the warrior replies. It is not the time for persuasive words.

'That belongs to the police,' Eaglehawk answers, trying to evade the reality. 'No white fellow policeman would allow me to take up a police gun to shoot him with. You're stupid, man!'

'Am I?' the outlaw grins. 'Am I?' he repeats. 'Shoot him and he can't say nothing. Then you have his gun. Right Captain?' he looks at Captain, the heavy Captain, far from his homeland, who can never be a leader.

The three tall powerful men stop in the middle of the red plain. Around them the hot breeze blows across their earth – soon to be taken from them for ever if they do not act.

'Shoot them,' Eaglehawk says in a daze. His mind clears: shooting is the beginning not the end! 'And when all my bullets are gone?' he questions, 'and when the police close around us, what then? Spears are like guns without bullets,' he sneers, the sneer of a man on the winning side.

'Get more bullets,' the practical Ellewara says – as quietly as the breeze. 'Fight them and take their bullets, more and more and more and more,' he shouts. There is no echo on the plains.

'Yes, but is it as easy as your words?' Eaglehawk queries, seeing the struggle before him, but wishing to avoid it.

'White men are lost in our land,' Ellewara whispers. 'They are easy to trap and kill. We'll raid their ugly houses, shoot them, kill them when and where they move. You can take all the bullets you need. More and more and more!'

The three men continue their march towards captivity. Eaglehawk feels a pain in his heart; his warrior scars feel taut and tight across his back and chest. Unconsciously his hand leaves the butt of his revolver to finger the stripes. He knows his land is fast becoming not his land; he knows he walks where the police order him to walk; he knows he is no longer a free man.

'Join us,' Ellewara insists. 'Join us, be men once again. All the best warriors of the tribes will follow you into the hills. You know the white man's ways. You know him and you can beat his every move. You belong to us and our earth. The white man is a foreigner, knowing neither us nor our land. How can he fight us if we stand together? We'll drive that fellow out and free our earth.'

Eaglehawk gestures angrily and to show his displeasure checks the warrior's handcuffs. The three stride on towards the homestead where the white boss waits.

III

Constable Richardson sits and watches his captives, five black men, six-footers, all with powerful barrel chests, heavy shoulders and sinewed for extreme endurance. Three are black bearded, the others clean shaven – by a razor made from a jagged flake of quartz or flint. Each man has speared at least one alien and are heroes throughout the Kimberleys. Heroes to the suppressed blacks-but to the young constable they are wild killers, devilishly cunning. He can't suppress a shudder when he thinks of their crimes. If they should get loose? He pushes the thought away and contemplates his success. He visualises the chevrons of a sergeant on his sleeve.

Everything has really gone splendidly – up to now – apart from the fever which saps his strength. But if his prisoners should get loose, here far from aid? He pushes the thought away. Almost singlehandedly, though with the help of Eaglehawk and Captain, he has managed to capture five of the most notorious native outlaws who have been creating trouble for years and have sworn to kill every white man they came across. Idle boasts now, but as he looks at them he shudders. There is still over 30 kilometres of rough country to the jail at Derby and on the way anything could happen. He examines the five. Their eyes are shadows under protruding brows and their teeth gleam in mocking smiles. He trembles and puts it down to the fever.

His prisoners look far too sure of themselves, too relaxed. What are they planning? He cannot understand these wild men; he can never begin to understand these so-called primitives who fill him with foreboding. He fumbles out his pipe. It falls from his shaking hand. Blaming the fever, he stares at the group of men.

They are tethered together by a long heavy chain looped about each prisoner's neck. The loop is not loose enough to enable a man to squirm his head through and not tight enough to choke him to death. Each loop of the chain is padlocked and the length of the links between each person is a regulation metre. Enough to allow room on the march. At halts, as now, one end of the chain is secured to a tree stump in the approved fashion. If a log, the desperate men might pick it up and jogtrot away into the darkness and freedom while the police constable and his trackers sleep. Then out of hearing, they would place the length of chain securing them to the log on a hard rock and pound away until a link flattened and parted. After that, a swift run into the sheltering hills, there to crouch among the rocks, each man pounding away at the chain midway between them until it parted. The young constable knows their tricks but he is frightened and sick with fever.

For over the twentieth time, though the sun has just risen, he peers towards the group, examining each man and trying to distinguish each padlock. From the verandah of the homestead, he looks down at the squatting black bodies, at Lillewara's face, clean shaven and intelligent: a face to watch, a man to watch. The black man, feeling the eyes on him, looks up and chuckles. The constable evades his eyes.

Three prisoners are curled up and appear asleep – but the constable knows this is the way they do their work best. Heads pillowed on their right arms, their agile fingers work on the padlocks. It only took one slinky gin to snake her way in during the night to throw a nail or a piece of wire among them. Then, as now, they would feign sleep while their nimble long fingers worked away, worked away.

He must not be careless, and the young constable, with promotion a certainty, has no intention of being careless. He gets to his feet and, loosening his revolver in its holster, steps off the verandah to talk to the prisoners. Standing a safe distance away, he orders them to their feet. The policeman scowls at Lillewara, Wongawara and Bundwan; at the blank face of Muckawara and the cheeky insolence of Luttawara. He orders each man to jerk the length of chain between them. He watches intently. His eyes seek out each padlock, each locked padlock. Satisfied he turns away.

Tired, anxious, eyes aching from lack of sleep, head spinning from fever, Constable Richardson waits for the return of his trackers. Along the verandah, up and down, he trudges. Then, at long last, with a sense of great relief, he makes out in the far distance, like a mirage, three figures moving towards the homestead. He shouts with joy when a glint of silver from the middle of a figure strikes his eye. It is Eaglehawk and Captain with Ellewara. Now at last a transfer south to Perth.

'Good, damn good, Eaglehawk,' he shouts as he runs to welcome them. 'Put the blighter on the chain, make certain of him.' He rubs his hands together in glee. He trusts his trackers. 'Get some tucker, as much as you want, you've more than earned it. After that, you'll both get a double ration of tobacco.'

Constable Richardson stands there gloating over his latest and most important prize. He is still smiling when the police tracker steps up and fires his pistol point blank into his face. His shattered face flashes red and his body convulses as it jerks to the ground. Sandawara lowers his gun. The white man twists into death at his feet. It is not an end, only a beginning. Sandawara puts aside all doubts and assumes command.

THREE

LEADERS AND FOLLOWERS

Alan steps back to study the slogan he's just tacked up on the wall. He straightens it, replaces the thumb tacks, then admires his work: DOPE'S DOPE. Sally and Jane stare at him.

One says to the other: 'What does it mean?'

'Silly, you know, what they were smoking last night when we came in.'

'Fags?'

'Dopy, pot!'

'Oh,' Jane says in incomprehension. Her restless eyes look around the room. 'Wish they had a telly. It's right on time for Cartoon Corner. They had one in the home.' She crawls to the edge of the mattress, searches through the litter on the floor and finds a comb. She begins combing her light brown hair. Sally tries to run her fingers through her hair, gets them entangled and snatches the comb from the other girl's hand. She tries to grab it back and they fall on to the mattresses and wrestle, their thin brown legs twisting around each other.

'Right kids,' Alan calls. Instantly they separate and watch him seriously.

'Rita, Rob,' Alan calls again, 'get Tom and Greg. They're at the back fixing the car. It's time for a session.'

The couple are in their territory, the kitchen, where Rob's trying his hand at kangaroo stew and dumplings. He wants to try something simple, something Rita can't spoil. Often he wishes that she wouldn't offer to help him every time. She's always brushing against him, and the kitchen table's becoming rickety from their constant screwing. He still has a blister on his arse from the time she fucked him right up against the stove. Today, he wanted to make Chilli Beef Brisket, but no one likes hot food except Gary who likes it too hot. Perhaps he'll try it tomorrow. It'd be a challenge. He stands stirring at the stove and Rita presses against his back, her hand snaking around to his cock. 'Honey,' he tells her, 'go around and call Tom and Greg, I've got to finish the stew.' He checks the gas jet to see if it's low enough and gives a start as Rita gives him one last squeeze. He lifts the lid off the pot. Rob's a finicky cook and spoils half the things he tries to make.

The girl taps him on the behind, right on the blister, before leaving. She passes Sue between the door and gate.

'Hi, Sue, how are you?' she grins. 'Hi, Rita, how's loverboy?'

'Cooking a terrific meal as usual.'

Sue flashes a grin and passes into the main room. Her face lights up as she sees Alan.

'Hi, I washed your shirt and socks. Got you a new pair of pants too. Hope you like washed denim?'

'Yeah, yeah, I just hope they aren't too light. I get around a lot and hate my things looking grubby,' Alan replies, giving her a broad smile. Recently, he's taken to posing in Sandawara style, his body taut as if ready to leap into conflict. He's beginning to exude a sense of power and destiny which will one day make him a leader of his people and a member of parliament. Now, catching the girl's joy at being with him, he settles into the pose. 'Thanks, I'll get into them now. You got here just in time for the session.'

'The session?' the girl queries, watching him strip. His thin, brown body emerges and she waits to see if he'll take it all off.

'Yeah, things've got to be tightened up. We're not a pack of bums, we're something else. Things have got to be talked over and settled once and for all,' the youth replies, hopping out of his pants, or trying to.

'Oh, that's what I was telling Tom just the other night. We've got to show them that we're not a pack of bloody boongs all on the grog. Here, let me untie your shoes for you. When you take off your trousers, remove your shoes first, it makes things a lot easier.' The girl bends to unlace his shoes and finds herself staring at his long brown cock only inches from her face. 'Lift up your foot a sec,' she says, breathlessly. She takes off his shoes. 'Now the other.' The girl pulls it off while watching the swing of his dick. Then, she realises where her eyes rest and jerks up, blushing.

'Our national costume,' the youth grins, posing nude in a spear-throwing attitude. His eyes go to the painting and he wishes for a full-length mirror to compare his stance.

'You're crazy,' Sue grins in return, slapping him on his hairless chest.

'Hey thanks, these pants are just right,' the youth says, pulling on the new trousers.

'Just right,' Sue replies. 'Hold still a minute.' She tears the label off the back and then takes her time in pulling out the thread. 'Good fit,' she adds and smacks him on the behind. 'I even washed Tom's clothes for him. Can't you get him to pull himself together? He's really letting himself go. Drunk every day.'

'I know, but it's better to go slowly. He's had it hard. Over east, he was in the can for two years.'

'I didn't know that.'

'He doesn't tell everyone. We have to be careful with him.'

'Uhuh, I see. I'll try and take it easy.'

'Hey, where're the others? Can't wait all arvo. I'll go and get them.'

He spins out of the room, and Sue goes over to sit with the two kids.

'Where're you from?'

'Narrogin,' they answer in unison.

'Where'd Alan find you?'

Sally looks at Jane, the spokeswoman of the two, and she answers: 'They had us in the remand centre and Alan was put in there. We nicked off with him.'

'What'd they put you in there for?'

Jane replies: 'They took us from mum and dad. Said we were running around wild. We were, too,' she grins. 'She's supposed to be pregnant.' Jane points at Sally.

'Are you?' Sue asks, studying the girl's figure.

'Dunno, they said I was. I don't feel anything.'

'Anyway, what are you two going to do?'

'Dunno,' they reply in unison, and Jane adds, 'Alan'll take care of us.'

'You don't want to go home?'

'What for? They'll only send us back,' Jane replies.

'Alan'll look after us,' Sally says.

They look at each other. Jane picks up the transistor and turns it on. The blur clears.

... His hair is long, his feet are hard and gritty,

He spends his life walking the streets of every city,

He's almost dead from breathing air pollution,

He doesn't vote, to him there's no solution:

Living just enough, just enough for the city.

'Give it here,' Sally mutters. 'That's no good.'

She tries to grab the radio off the girl and it goes dead. Both girls begin wrestling. Charly stumbles in, looking as if he's on a week long drunk. His eyes have receded right into his head under the beetling brows; his hair is matted, and his clothing is rumpled and stained. Without a word to the three girls, he reaches for the guitar, strums the strings and begins to tune them. They watch as he strums a chord to his satisfaction, then begins to sing.

A gallant black stockman lay dying,
With his saddle supporting his head,
And around him his gins were lying,
When he rose on his elbow and said:

Oh, there's rum in the old battered billy,
Lay the pannikins all in a row,
And we'll booze to the next happy meeting
In the land where all good blackies go.

While he's singing, the others come in, smile or grin and shove on to the mattresses. Tom and Greg are smudged with oil. Tom tries to squash in between the wall and Sue. She isn't having any and makes him change his mind with an angry gesture. Alan stands waiting in the middle of the room. A bundle of energy, he's ready to get the session under way, but politely waits until Charly is through.

So wrap me up in my stockwhip and blanket,
And bury me deep down below,
Where the boss and the wife can't molest me,
In that land where all us blackies go.

'God, he'll give us *Waltzing Matilda* next,' Greg whispers, looking towards Rita for some return to his words. He receives none and scowls.

Sue looks at Tom and grimaces: 'I've washed some clothes for you. Have a shower first before you put them on. You know, there's hot water here.'

'Didn't know that,' Tom scowls in turn.

Then Rob enters from the kitchen and Rita gestures him to her side. She immediately leans on him and puts her hand on his thigh. Greg mutters something and moves closer to the teenybopper, Jane. Both girls look at him.

'Where're you from?' Jane whispers to him. He looks almost as young as they do, or at least they think he does.

'From York way,' he whispers back suddenly, in spite of his bulk, looking sixteen.

'We went through there once, didn't think much of it,' Jane answers roughly. She knows the sort of lady she wants to grow into and practises the part.

Charly has grown silent. He flops down in a corner and appears to go to sleep.

Alan poses in front of Sandawara and says: 'We're all here, about time. How's the transport shaping up, Greg?' He stares at the youth.

'The bastard's ready to move, but the registration'll be out in a day or two.'

'Get Gary to renew it. We can't be without wheels when we need them.'

'He's getting dicy about his car,' Tom puts in. 'He complains that we're taking it over.'

'So we are,' Alan answers with a laugh. 'We're fixing it and we can use it. If he doesn't like it, let him talk to Greg about it.'

Greg grins. Gary's in mortal dread of him. 'Yeah, let him,' he sneers. 'It would've cost him over a hundred bucks to get it fixed at a garage.'

Rob disengages Rita, leaps up and dashes into the kitchen to take care of his stew. 'Grub's just about ready,' he calls, coming back. 'You'll like it you will – real bush tucker.'

'Right,' Alan orders. He steps to his slogan and stands beside it. 'The other night when I got back I found you all smoking pot. If I'd a been a cop, it would've been a bust and the end of my setup. And what if Ron catches on? You know what he's like!' He stares at each in turn. 'You know, I'm trying to get things together for all of us and you go and do a dumb thing like that. I've tried that poison; it slowed me right down, and I couldn't even think straight. That's the reason why I don't like it. You can't work when you smoke it. All you can do is lie around all day stupid! Tom, you're on the grog, why'd you want to take the other? But I'll let you pass for the time being.

Drink if you want to, but no dope, understand? We've got to be very careful. I don't want my plans fucked up.' He stares at Greg who looks away. 'You Greg, haven't you tried to work on the car after smoking a joint? How much work did you do?' He waits for an answer.

Muscles tries to look thoughtful: 'Not much, but I was thinking things out.'

'Yeah,' Alan grins, then continues: 'What about you, Rob? You're a good cook' – Rob happily smiles – 'and you feed us real good, but we can all remember the time you and Rita were smoking and the burnt mess you tried to dish us up.'

The youth looks hurt and his girl friend caresses his side under his shirt.

'As for you, Rita,' Alan says, raising his voice. The girl pulls out her hand and waits for the worst. 'You got any of it left?' He stares at the girl. She nervously searches for her boy friend's hand and holds on.

'Right, hand it over!' Alan commands.

Although this has happened before, the others watch for a sign of revolt. But the girl gives in, feels under a mattress, tugs out her stash bag and flings it to Alan who catches it. He holds it up. 'You want to be dopes; you want to give those pigs who trade in this stuff money to harm yourselves? You want to do what they want you to do? If you do, go right ahead, but not near me. I'm not going to be dopy or watch you making dopes out of yourselves either. Do we need this poison? No!' He stares into each face. Only one person can meet his eyes – Sue, and she gazes in admiration, a political groupie. Fancy a kid acting like this and the others taking it.

'Here, Sue,' Alan calls, tossing the cloth bag to her. 'Burn it!'

'Good, Alan,' the girl replies, getting up and going to the fireplace in a corner of the room. She crumbles some paper, finds a box of matches in the rubbish on the floor (she'll clean up the place one day), sets the paper ablaze and puts the bag on top. The kids watch. It was good dope.

'Right, let's hope that scene is over for good,' Alan recalls their attention. He resumes his Sandawara pose, his body taut and straight. The only thing lacking is the rifle held like a spear. 'And so we don't need this.' He rips the sign DOPE'S DOPE off the wall. 'No one's a dope around here.' He grins at Greg who for some reason feels that he is being got at. 'We're not dopes, are we?' Alan says, still looking at Greg.

'Not me,' the youth declares. 'I never liked that stuff. I like other things, like fixing the car or having a good blue.'

Tom stares at the fire, then at the door. His mouth's dry; he wants a drink, but has stashed his bottle in the shithouse. He thinks things are getting heavier and heavier. Sue watches him licking his lips. He suddenly says: 'Hey, Rob, I'm hungry, is the stew ready?'

'Yeah,' the cook instantly replies and gets to his feet. 'I'll dish it up.'

'I'll help you,' Tom says with a rush.

Rita follows the cook out to the kitchen, but Tom charges off to the shithouse. After a long swig he feels much better. Give him a bottle of wine any day. He empties the bottle before he knows it then, a little unsteady on his feet, goes to the kitchen to help carry the bowls of stew in to the others. Trying to sit down with his bowl, he almost falls and splashes his pants. Sue glares at him, but he doesn't deign to notice. It isn't any of that bitch's business anyway!

'Man, this is so much better than your other slop,' the jealous Greg digs at Rob, wanting to hurt. He receives a glare from Rita and looks towards Jane and winks. The teenybopper winks back. She thinks Greg's great and much better than the others, though Alan's the greatest.

'Think I'll have a shower,' Tom blurts out. He's tried a few spoonfuls of the stew and feels the urge to vomit.

'You do that,' Sue says, handing him a plastic carrybag and catching a whiff of his breath. 'Have a long one, it'll do you good,' she calls after his back, then catches Alan's eyes and feels bad for what she's just said.

Jane and Sally finish off their bowls of stew and accept the offer of refills from the cook. Happily, he watches them spoon it down. Lunch over, they look about for something to interest them. They wish for a telly or even a record machine, not what these big kids are putting across.

'Hurry up, Tom,' Greg shouts out above the rush of the shower. 'I want one, too.' He grins at Jane who winks back. To impress her, he picks up the radio, pulls the back off and proceeds to take it apart. Both kids crawl nearer to watch.

Alan begins scribbling on a sheet of paper as Rita and Rob collect the bowls and make off to the kitchen to do some making out. The youth has difficulty writing and Sue, who has studied past primary school, goes across to help him. She sits right against him, pressing into his side as she takes the paper and waits for dictation. Alan feels the softness of her breast against his arm, but forgets her as a girl as he begins explaining what he wants to put down.

II

The shower's changed Tom for the better. In a clean shirt and jeans and with his hair neatly combed, the scruffy down-and-out looks almost presentable, as if he's holding down a job paying good money. Even his head's been cleared of drunkenness.

'Right Tom,' Alan says, looking at him with approval, and even Sue has a smile for him. All in all, Tom feels a little different, not so negative, not so much the Nungar who can't help being dirty and drunken. 'Right Tom,' Alan says again. 'I've just been working on something with Sue,' he grins at the girl and Tom can't help seeing her answering smirk. 'Yes, Sue and me have drafted a letter. What Perth needs is a Nungar youth centre. Someone'll get around to doing it sooner or later, but I want to get in and try to do it first.' He almost glows. 'We kids should organise our own centre, then I'll have a real base. Just imagine fifty kids all living together, wouldn't that be something? Fifty kids to train, to get them together to fight back.'

Tom's unfamiliar positive thoughts have left and he's flopped back beside the two teenyboppers, now he leaps into a sitting position. 'Fight back? What's this fighting back supposed to mean?'

'I've talked about it often enough,' Alan replies quietly, too confident to be taken for a kid of sixteen. 'Look, now if the pigs pick us up, who cares? Just the other day they got me, and what could I do? Nothing! It was their scene all the way. Well, just put this in your head. Say you're busted for nothing, right? And then there's fifty of us demonstrating outside the pigsty. Just think of that!' His eyes turn towards the painting of Sandawara. 'And who knows where it'll end?'

'Kidstuff,' Tom jeers from his maturity of twenty-five. 'They'll only see you as a lot of troublemakers and close the hostel quick-smart.'

The budding leader takes up the challenge. 'Maybe, maybe, but something could come out of it. Something will come out of it. They'll see only a bunch of kids just as you do, but we ain't exactly that. I've been on the streets since I was nine and I've had my eyes and ears open and I've had them opened. I've picked up a lot.'

'Yeah, so have I,' Tom grins, refusing to take it seriously, 'a lot of bottles.' Sue glares at him, his face closes up and he feels the urge for another drink. This kid's far too heavy for him with all his scheming and plotting. 'Well, I've been here, there and everywhere since I was a kid and I ain't exactly dumb myself, but street living never helped me much.'

'Anyway,' Alan continues, ignoring the man's words, 'I'm going down to see Ken Rawlings and have a talk with him. He won't listen to a kid like me, but you're older and he might listen to you. At least, we'll get some facts out of him, who to contact and things like that. Who knows, he might even put in a good word for us.' His dream carries him away. 'Just think of it, fifty blokes all ready for action, any time, anywhere. Man, it'll be like an army, that will.'

'Yeah, but you know Rawlings, he's so straight, so much the black leader, and he wants to keep everything right in his own hands. He won't like street bums coming to him with smart ideas. If anything, he'll pinch it and take all the credit.'

'You don't get anywhere if you don't try,' the kid snaps. 'We might get some good ideas from him.'

'From him?' Tom sneers. 'Just scratch him and it's all lilywhite under that black skin of his.'

'Maybe, maybe,' Alan replies. 'We'll try it and if we get nothing, there's always other ways.'

'For us, what do you want us to do, rob a bank?'

'Why not?' Alan says. 'Why not?'

The two teenyboppers, who've been all ears though little understanding, nudge each other and stare at Alan. He's the greatest and where all the action is. Tom and Sue glance at each other. They haven't been prepared for this, and don't know what to make of it. Alan did get the craziest ideas, then perhaps it wasn't so mad. A silence falls. Then quietly, stealthily, like a ghost materialising, Ron appears in the doorway. No one notices him.

Alan continues: 'You know, I've heard about this bloke in Russia, Joe Stalin. He was just like us and later on he became boss of all the USSR. But before that, one time him and his mob wanted money, not for themselves, but to use in the fight against the pigs. The only way he could get it was by robbing a bank. He did just that. If you want money for something good and go out and take it, it ain't stealing, it's liberating what's rightfully yours. Well, old Joe Stalin was never a crook, he was a hero fighting for his people. If he could get a start that way, so can we!'

'But Alan,' Sue protests, then changes what she was about to say, 'we might get caught and that'll be the end of everything. They'll put us in jail.'

'I hate jail,' Tom breaks in bitterly. 'I hate being locked up like some kind of animal. I don't want any part of it. All I want out of life is a bottle of booze and a place to crash. The dole's enough for me. If they arrest you for being drunk, it's only a fine, but for robbing a bank they put you away for years and years, not for one or two days.'

'Yeah, that's if we get caught and who's going to get caught? Do you really want to be a dole bludger all your life? Don't you want to be part of something that'll really help your people. Haven't you got the guts to stand up and be counted?'

'I don't like jail,' Tom replies doggedly to Alan. 'I get by all right. I don't want to be a big wheel.'

'Hey,' Sue breaks in. 'Alan, you're a juvenile and it'll be my first big offence. They'll only put you in a home till you're eighteen and I'll get probation, won't I?'

'No worries, mate,' Alan says, radiating reassurance. 'No worries at all. We've got it made and we're not going to be caught anyway.'

'Yeah,' Tom exclaims bitterly, 'but what about me? I'm twenty-five and besides ...' he breaks off. He doesn't want Sue to know that he's been inside.

Alan and Sue exchange glances. The man thinks they're putting him down for being yellow and cries out: 'O.K., O.K., anything, but it doesn't mean we're going to do it, does it?'

Alan glances sideways and starts as he sees Ron standing, listening. 'No, it's only a joke, kidstuff,' he laughs; the others follow the direction of his eyes and find Ron. 'Come in, Ron, and sit down. Heard you had a little trouble the other night,' Alan says.

The man slides further into the room, then deliberately submits the interior to a long searching study. He sees Charly in the corner and goes and sits as far away as he can. 'Yeah, that Gary,' he mumbles out, 'that wog,' he snarls. Charly moves into a more aware position and Ron gives a shudder, as if expecting something not nice from him. He almost cringes as the youth staggers to his feet and without a word wanders past him, too close for comfort, and out of the room.

'That bloke's crazy,' Ron whispers. 'You know, he was a boxer. Now he's punchy, out of his head. When he gets enough grog in him, he loses his block and starts lashing out. They put him in the can for almost killing someone. Why'd you let him in here? He's crazy!' Then he stares at the two teenyboppers who, terrified though deliciously, huddle against each other, eyes big. 'Why're they here? Who are they? Where did they come from?' the man jerks out. 'What's happening to this place? Does Gary know they're here? He's particular, he is. He lets me come in here, but he doesn't like little kids hanging around. Too much trouble, and that wog doesn't like trouble.' He leers in their direction. 'Anything could happen to them here, you know that Charly ...'

'Ron,' Alan breaks in, 'this is a refuge. A crashpad. Anyone can come and stay for a few days and get themselves together. Anyone! – so you have to learn and live with them, learn and live with all sorts.'

'Yeah, yeah,' the man agrees, eyeing the girls and almost licking his lips. His mind switches: 'Where's that Greg?'

'Having a shower,' Tom grins. 'He'll be finished soon. You got that thirty cents you owe him? He didn't like what you did the other night, and the bricks on the roof made him real mad.'

Ron forgets the girls as he becomes alarmed. 'He's a bad bastard, he is. One of these days I'll take a knife to him, I will just wait and see. And as for that Gary, I'll burn the place down.' His mind switches back, and he throws a sinister grin towards the little girls. 'What're your names?' Their frightened look, with a feeling of enjoyment about being scared, turns him on. He begins a slow creep towards them.

'Ron, you'll have to cool it,' Alan says hurriedly, but with a smile. He's confident he can handle the man. 'We're all mates here and help each other.'

'Yeah, all mates, though I don't know about Greg,' Tom grins. 'All right for both of yous,' the man snarls, 'no one calls me mate. You know what mates are like? They suck up to you, and the next thing you know they've done the dirty on you. I know mates I do!' Ron's almost at the edge of the mattresses, though none of the people present can work out his means of locomotion. 'Yeah,' he goes on, 'they don't even like giving you the time of day, let alone twenty cents for a cup of coffee. Fuck everyone, that's what I say.' Ron's almost in reaching distance of the girls and they watch him, much as a rabbit watches a snake, or the killer the hangman. The man fumbles in his pocket, finds a coin and looks at it: two cents! Alan's face is reflected in his sunglasses for a second as he turns to him, then he hears the sound of the shower being turned off.

Alan adds to Ron's apprehension by saying: 'We're just about ready to go out. Look, Tom's had his first shower and change of clothing in a month. You want to come along with us, or stay with Greg until we get back?'

The plan works. The man's terrified of Greg. One moment, he's sitting on the floor ready to reach for Sally, the next he's on his feet mumbling about how he'll get everyone some day, then he's gone.

This time the door slams and the gate.

'Man, he scares me,' Sue breathes out, 'though I know he's not for real. He's like something you find haunting the graveyard.'

'Arrh, he's lonely. He comes here because there's no other place that'll stand him. But he's harmless, I think,' Alan stops, not entirely certain.

'Yeah, he's harmless,' Tom says. 'One time I was pissed and they flung me out of this place. I came across Ron, and you know how he's always talking about getting even with some bloke or burning the place down? So I put the question to him. I wanted to burn that hotel right down to the ground, but he wouldn't be in it.'

'That was a stupid thing to do,' Sue cuts in. 'Much more stupid than robbing a bank.'

'Yeah, yeah,' Tom growls, needled. 'Anyway, you better watch out, he likes little girls.'

'I'm not so little.'

'So, you're saved for a fate worse than Ron.'

Sally and Jane listen with bated breath. Everything's so groovy and exciting, if only there was a telly.

'Well, he won't be back for a day or two,' Alan says, 'he's shit scared of Greg.'

'And Charly,' Tom puts in. 'Then, he doesn't like any of us much.'

'Not many of those Aussie blokes do, but it's good having him around. Just goes to show us what they're really like. Right, let's go and see Rawlings,' Alan commands, springing to his feet.

'Yeah, let's go,' agrees Tom, slowly getting to his feet. He could use a drink.

III

The two teenyboppers sit on the mattress, very, very bored. To break the monotony, Jane begins rapping to Sally, trying to put her into a television dreamland. 'And you know, this plane's crashed. It isn't one of those great big ones, just a little one. It comes swooping down on the snow. Something breaks and it can't get off the ground. Even Lassie tries her best and can't do a thing. She does pull a bloke out of the plane, but that's all. Then finally, the pilot manages to get the plane into the sky. It wobbles going along the snow, then just before reaching a cliff edge, it takes off, like this. Gee, I left out the main thing – Lassie has to be left behind.'

'Why?' a confused Sally demands.

'I don't know why, dummy, she just has to be left behind. Anyway, she's left behind, tied between two sticks. You'll see why in a moment. Then the plane swoops out of the sky and Lassie barks up a hello. Behind the plane's a long rope with an iron hook on the end. The hook grabs Lassie's lead and she's hoisted up in the air. It doesn't hurt her one bit. You should've seen her dangling in the air. Still, Lassie isn't scared. No, not that dog. Nothing can scare Lassie!'

'I'd have been scared out of my pants,' Sally cuts in as Jane falters in her storytelling.

'So would I have been; but we ain't Lassie. Just about everything happens to that dog, and she's used to it. Like it's her job and so she don't get frightened like you or me would. Anyway, she just hangs there on the end of that long rope. Just dangling there and being pulled in towards the side of the plane. She wags her tail as she nears. Then they pull her through a window or door, I forget which, and she starts licking the pilot's face. Wish I had a dog like Lassie. You didn't see it on telly, did you? Well, you should have!'

Greg's gone to the kitchen to make coffee and has driven Rita and Rob apart. Rob's glad to escape from his girl friend's arms. He's anxious about what to prepare for the early morning meal, and so far has only thought of spaghetti. Part of the proceeds of the store robbery, has been two dozen packets, and he doesn't want to waste them. If he does use them, he can make the nice sauce he's found the recipe for in an old magazine.

Muscles stamps about the cramped kitchen space. He disturbs everything as much as possible as he puts the water on to boil, takes out the mugs and adds milk and sugar to them. He pours the boiling water into the mugs and stirs it before remembering the coffee. He spoons it on top and stirs it in.

'That's not the way to make coffee,' Rob looks on in horror. 'It should be done with the coffee, then the boiling water's added, followed by the milk and sugar.'

'Arrh, who cares a stuff,' Greg snarls as he takes up the mugs and exits with a smouldering anger at the injustice of such a guy getting it off with a chick like Rita – and not only once, but all the time. It's beyond his understanding and he flexes his muscles to rebuild his confidence. He likes the two kids in the other room. No fucking about with them at all, just kids that like fun. Greg enters the room and strides to the girls, grinning.

'Coffee, girls?'

He gives each a mug, then sits at the side of Jane. 'How you going?'

'Righto, I guess, but we've been sitting here all arvo. Nothing to do. If only there was a telly.'

'We'll find something to do,' the youth answers, putting his arm around the girl and giving her a hug.

Jane giggles: 'Hey, don't get fresh!'

'Who's getting fresh? I like you, and you've done it before, haven't you?'

'Done what?' the girl says smugly. She looks at Sally and both go into a fit of giggling.

'You know what,' Greg insists.

'So what,' Jane giggles. 'Let me drink my coffee.'

A morose Gary comes in and scowls at the three. The world's sitting more and more heavily on his shoulders. He wants to get the Abos out of his pad; he wants his pad for himself, and he wants to protect his lovely '66 Holden; but how can he when the others have all the muscle power? The conflict wrinkles his young forehead. More and more of ten, he is beginning to feel like going home to Mum and Dad. But his father's an ex-Indian army major starting anew in a foreign colony and lectures his son on the worthlessness of his life and prays for him to enroll in the airforce. Naturally, his son's appalled at the prayer; he's all for peace and love, but now with Alan and his mob turning the pad heavy with impending violence, the airforce seems the more peaceful environment. Automatically he stares at Greg and shudders: that guy can do anything; then he sees the girls and the idea of fleeing leaves his mind: a crashpad does have its advantages. Greg's taken over the more loquacious Jane, leaving the quieter Sally, but she's starting to develop a good pair of tits. He sits beside her, and the girl welcomes him. Jane's been getting all the attention and she's feeling out of it.

'Hi, Gary, where have you been?' a happier Greg calls across the two girls.

Gary hasn't been anywhere in particular (he fled the pad to escape the heavy vibes and wandered around a park), but he answers very togetherlike: 'Band business. Getting the group together. In a week we'll try for some gigs. This guy's offered to come in as a bass guitarist.'

The groupie in Sally turns into big eyes and Jane bursts out in rapture: 'You're a singer in a band. Which one?'

Instantly, Gary goes into his nonchalant such-is-fame role: 'Last group, The Mouldy Curs, folded in a month. Now I'm getting a new band together, a disco group. We'll play all happy music.' He puffs out his chest. 'I'll be the lead guitarist and singer. Greg there'll be the drummer.'

To add to his impression, Gary reaches along the wall to his guitar. He gets to his feet while Greg searches the mess on the floor for his drumsticks. He taps the sticks together as Gary goes into his routine. He takes two steps forward, two steps back as he hits a chord on his box, hunches over slightly and whines out in a not too unpleasant voice:

Take the money and run,
Take the money and run,
Take the money and run,
Find a place and have some fun.

He hits a wrong chord and clangs to a halt. Greg pounds away for a few bars, then trails off. The boys look at the girls and find them suitably impressed.

'You wait till we have the whole group blasting,' the guitarist singer promises. 'Then, it'll be pow, right to the top forty.'

'I get my drum kit next week,' the projected drummer of the future group shouts, his hands steadily banging out a shuffling disco beat.

Sally and Jane look at each other, then at the boys. For a long moment, they wish to be back in the remand home where they can brag about the groovy people they've met, even the spooky Ron would be good for a scare; but only for a moment, for the boys of the band are off again. The guitarist strikes a chord, the drummer sets the rhythm, and the two bang and strum along for another few minutes.

Greg bangs fiercely, showing his skill. He's determined to be the drummer, but afraid of being conned out of his dream. Then, he has doubts about the guitar playing ability of Gary. For his money, Charly plays better than the wog. Perhaps when he gets his drum set, he and Charly could form a country and western group and play at the pubs. Just a few hundred bucks for equipment and he'll be home. Gary strums another wrong chord and stops. Greg sighs, and remembers the car. 'Hey, I've fixed the car, let's take it on a spin.'

'Are you sure you fixed it?' replies the cautious Gary. After all it is his vehicle.

'Yeah, yeah, it's running like a bomb. Even put a radio in.'

'Where'd you get it? Hope it ain't hot.'

'Never you mind. You needed it and I got it. I'm always picking up bits and pieces.' He squeezes Jane and gets a giggle. 'You want to come along, don't you?'

'We both want to go,' the girls answer in unison.

'But I haven't got a licence,' Gary squeals out: he doesn't like the idea at all.

'Don't worry, mate,' Greg grins. 'We'll head for the bush, no pigs out there.'

'I don't know if Alan would go for it. You know, he doesn't like us acting dumb.'

'Arrh, he won't mind,0Æ Greg says, putting down the appeal to authority, 'and the kids want some air, don't you girls?'

'Yeah, it'll be dark before you know it,' the confident Jane agrees, leaping to her feet, instantly followed by Sally. Gary reluctantly trails the others from the room. The airforce is beginning to have even more appeal to him.

IV

The new washed and clean Tom feels up to being the spokesman of the group. Even his brain, for once, is clear enough to be used, and he sifts through the different convicts he met in jail, trying to find a sophisticated personality to assume for the occasion. With some trepidation, he finally settles into the personality of a prison welfare officer who once tried to befriend him, to help him, to give him up finally, not as a bad case, but as a hopeless one. Tom speaks, trying for sincerity plus:

'Well, sir, we know that you're very busy and we hate disturbing you; but you know, we Nungar kids, I mean young people – there's no place for us to live and work together and so, we run wild, without guidance.' He trails off, conscious that he hasn't done a good job.

Alan, who knows he can do it better and who doesn't like being upstaged, even badly, breaks out: 'Sir, what we need, to tell you the truth, is a youth centre run by the kids themselves. You know, as in the slogan: FOR YOUTH, BY YOUTH. That sums it up completely – except that we're willing to accept outside guidance. We know we need it, at least for the beginning. Don't you see that there's a crying need for kids like ourselves to have some place we can call home? Where we can go and feel completely relaxed.' The youth knows his man, and he finishes off with: 'We want to be self-reliant, we want to do things for ourselves, not always having someone else telling us to do this, do that. We want to be like you and stand on our own two feet.'

The conservative Aboriginal leader, sitting across from them, smiles as he hears the last words. At last his message is getting across. He smiles again as he leans forward. There's no desk except a psychic one. Ken Rawlings puts the tops of his fingers together and leans his elbows on that imaginary desk, as he waits for them to continue – waiting, consciously attentive. He's a leader of his people and from the people. His clothing and body are rough, those of a working man, and his face, the heavy brows, the deepset eyes, the jowls together with the wild crop of black hair, are all there and real; but to the young people in front of him, he's not for real, not a symbol of themselves – though he could be.

Rawlings is on the way to a safe seat in parliament and has listened to

Alan's plea with a slight sense of being upstaged. He thinks over his reply. As a forthcoming politician he has a supply of platitudes which can be trotted forth. He, too, is sincere, in a homely fashion, in a straightforward fashion that curves and zigzags. He talks straight, man to man, with his big eyes shining like twin pools under overhanging cliffs. He thrusts forward with an attentiveness, with a wish to please. His party finds him an asset on the platform, a symbol of Australia; but to the boys he's heavy and inert. The solid hand of adult authority. He's made it and knows it, and to these kids, that's somehow a sellout.

'I know mates,' the leader begins, in his deep authoritative, but friendly voice, in his deep but compromising voice. He holds all the cards and as an experienced player can deal them how he wishes and when he wishes. His words roll out and his eyes move from person to person. Alan is all ears, the perfect pupil. 'Now, you know and I know that over the last years, we've been slowly and surely making our way into the mainstream of Australian society. More and more, we're becoming accepted, not as inferiors, but as equals.'

Rawlings stops, hoping that he's not been too political and obtuse with these kids, but a look at Alan's rapt face (he so loves a cliché) makes him go on with joy: 'Just like any other citizen in Australia, we have our rights, equal rights with every other person. Everyone's the same as us, mate, all Aussies, and don't you forget that. You know, I met this Nungar bloke today. He got his own truck and is doing contract work and getting jobs too! That's progress, mate; that's how we earn respect. Not by lying around, not by thinking that the state owes us a living, but by good, honest, hard work.' The leader stops, his deepset eyes judging the impact.

Alan feels like clapping. He honestly likes it, but Tom is bored though careful not to show it: his opinion, a blowhard!

Rawlings goes on, his voice changing to sadness: 'That's the good part, but sadly, very sadly, there's the other part, and I dislike saying this, but some of the old people – well, they like the odd drop of wine, and if they'd only go off and have it at home or in the bush or in a derelict house but, no, they don't do that. They drink in an alley, a park, a doorway, and next thing you see is one of our blokes dead-drunk in the street, staggering all over the place and bringing disgrace down on us. This really hurts our image. How can we show the white people what we are, when they only have to go along certain Perth streets to see this disgrace? And not quiet streets, but main roads like Beaufort and William. Now, at last, I've got a shelter where they can be taken to sober up and be given a good feed, but the problem's still there. Mark me, there'll come a day when these old blokes can be kept from giving a bad example and being a bad example to the Nungar folk. One day, you just mark my words, if my party gets in, we'll have an old folk's home where we can put them. That's a step in the right direction, that is, and that's what is needed. A nice home for the old fellows, like the white blokes have, but one with a bit more bush around it.'

For some time the upstaged Alan's been visibly squirming, like a young kid who wants to leave the room and is too frightened to ask, and now, in an effort to get the ball under his command, he breaks in with 'Yes, sir, that's fine for the old folks, but what about the up-and-coming generation, the voters of tomorrow? You know, we're all for a good deal for the old blokes, it'll keep them off the streets, but we also want to be kept off the streets. You know, we're young and interested mainly in our own age group.'

Alan has captured the ball, now Tom accepts a pass: 'Sir, we're interested in having a youth centre established in Perth. We think the time has come for such a centre to be established and that the youth are mature enough to run it themselves.' He looks across at Sue and shoots her the ball.

Sue accepts it: 'You, sir, have seen for yourself how hard the kids worked in collecting signatures on the Aboriginal Land Rights petition. We supported the cause of our country brothers and sisters in that; now we feel that we can be more active in helping the urban Nungars.'

The girl streaks for the goal. She's certain the leader's noticed her around his centre helping out – but she's afraid that the man will block her by assuming the others are idlers and bludgers with a silly scheme. This is what the leader does, or almost. He finds the idea sound, but dismisses the delegation, except for Sue and the little one who, he senses, could turn out to be something in a few years. Rawlings decides to soothe them, then send them away. Attentively, he faces Sue as she prepares to shoot for goal.

'Sir, we've drawn up a letter showing the type of hostel and centre we would like to run and have for a Nungar youth place.' She hands him the letter Alan and she had drawn up back at the pad. The man holds the letter in his big worker's hands, opens it with thick fingers, bends his wild haired Nungar head and runs his dark eyes over the few lines that the kids have written out, all legal-like.

Sir,

We, the undersigned, on behalf of the Nungar youth of Perth and Western Australia, feel that a youth centre and hostel should be established for our welfare and well-being – there being no such centre in Perth, as yet. We, herewith, would like you, sir, to apply to the proper governmental authority for a grant which will enable us to establish the needed centre and hostel as quickly as possible. For our purpose, we need:

A. A large building with space for 30 or 40 persons to sleep and with cooking and dining facilities.

B. A large hall to be equipped as a gymnasium and martial arts centre.

C. A large open space for games and other events.

As we, the undersigned, do not have the means to buy or lease and equip such a centre, we wish you, Sir, to apply to the government for a grant-in-aid.

Thanking you, on behalf of the Nungar Youth,

Alan Mitchell
Tom Johnson
Sue Michaels
Greg Toll
Rob Sampy
Rita Yarrie

The delegation of the Nungar youth of Perth and Western Australia wait, their eyes on the big black man who now raises his head. He recognises the hand of Sue in the letter. She's done some typing for his New Action Centre and learnt the format. He allows the game to close with a point to the opposing team. 'Yes, yes,' he says, suddenly feeling official under the eyes of the delegation. It's the first time such a delegation has come to him and he feels elevated: this'll be what it'll be like being an M.P. 'Well, mates,' he says, very much the cheery politician. 'It's a blooming good idea, but I'll have to map it out properly before putting it before the Community Welfare Department in Canberra. And I can tell you in confidence that cash is pretty short now, what with inflation and unemployment. I'll tell you what I'll do. I'll put the project before the committee of my centre and see what they think of it. I won't promise anything, but if it's approved, I'll back it in Canberra. But remember, slow and steady wins the race. And I'm sure,' his big sincere eyes reach out to each in turn, 'we'll be able to find a place in this scheme for you. It's heartwarming to find people, especially young folk, that want to help themselves and others. It's the only way to succeed. Self-help, the will to get ahead. You know, when I was your ages, I was a real bush Nungar. I didn't even know how to read or write, then I took a few lessons and almost taught myself.'

He sweeps one large hand around the hall in which they're sitting. 'See this, I began it. Got the money from the government and put the place together almost with my own hands.' He indicates the office partition at one end of the hall. 'Bookkeeping and typing, I learnt them.' He points a thick finger at a stage at the far end. 'We decided to put on some plays with Nungar themes. Not only have I written one, I've staged it. I had to learn all about lighting, directing, producing – the lot. And you know what then?' The leader stares in each face. All, especially Alan, are rapt. Alan's learning. 'I taught others to do what I could do. And that's what I like. Self-help and then helping others to lift themselves by their bootstraps as I've done.' He indicates the stage again. 'We're planning to put on a short piece I have written, in a few days time. It's about the first meeting between the Nungars and the whites. I show the two races meeting and how they, through misunderstanding and sheer accident, become enemies. It's a sad, sad story,' the man says, shaking his head, and rising to his feet. The others do so too. 'Well,' the leader says, looking into each face, 'thanks for your idea. I'll see what I can do.' He remembers their names. 'Righto, goodbye Sue, Tom and Alan. I've got to go and pick up the kids from school.' He shakes hands and walks off with a walk slowly turning dignified. Already, his hair's grey in parts – going with maturity, self government and reliance.

'A lot of bullshit makes the world go round,' Tom observes: his stomach sour for a drink turning his mind sour.

'He's got some good ideas,' Alan says with fervour.

'He's really done a lot for us,' Sue adds.

'And for himself,' Tom says, cynically, 'but that's how the world is.'

'One day it'll change,' Alan declares firmly: 'No compromise!'

Tom can almost see his fist shoot up, and smiles and replies: 'We just did, that is if we didn't get the old brush off. One thing's for certain, if the youth centre gets off the ground, we won't be running it.'

'Maybe,' the aspiring leader says, deep in thought. 'Maybe if we go along with him we can get what we want eventually. You know, we have to have a hand in running things, and then, slowly,' he grins, 'slow and steady wins the race, we take control.'

'Oh yeah,' Tom grins. 'They're sure to have some sort of goody-goody in charge with a direct line to the nearest cop shop.'

'Maybe,' Alan slowly says. 'Maybe. Should we wait and see what happens?'

'And he is interested,' adds Sue, trying to put the best face on things.

'Of course, he is,' Tom jeers. 'It's a better idea than his old folks' home. God, they'll be putting us in concentration camps soon, just to keep the image shining. Fuck them,' he snarls, turning bitter. He needs a drink badly and tries to think of an excuse for ducking into the nearest pub.

Alan's eyes reach out to his favourite paintings. Six oils hung high on both the long walls. Metre squares of masonite painted a hot dusty, dry yellow orange red of the desert heart of Australia. Dotted white lines centre rushing streaks of black circling in the abstract mythic pattern of the sacred dance. Resembling, but not copies of, bark paintings, the pictures are modern, black and Australian.

'Man, he's the only painter I dig,' Alan almost whispers, his face lifted to the sacred scenes.

'I like this Sandawara one the best,' Tom says and wants to go on sarcastically, but loses his inclination when he sees how immersed Alan is in Rebel's work. 'Really mod art,' he finishes with a bit of eastern sophistication which doesn't come off. He hasn't been in an art gallery in his life, nor have any of the others. They aren't art freaks.

'Man,' Alan goes on, 'every time I see them I think of how we could use them in the crashpad. Might come down one night and rip them off.'

'Oh Alan,' Sue remonstrates, 'these are ours. This is our place, a Nungar place!'

'Yeah, yeah,' he replies. His mind flickers away. 'Say, let's go to Obelia's and have a coffee. They have good sounds there.'

'Not like Gary,' Tom smiles, 'or Charly for that matter.'

His urge for a drink makes Tom quickly agree: there's a pub a few doors from Obelia's.

'But Alan,' Sue almost wails, 'we haven't decided what to do about the youth centre.'

'Don't worry,' he calls back to her. 'Things'll work out. We'll get the money from another source. We'll ask the bank for a loan.'

'But Alan,' the girl cries, 'they won't give us one.'

'Want to bet,' Alan grins over his shoulder at her.

Tom, walking at his side, suddenly doesn't like the subject. He feels walls closing in on him and desperately wants that drink. Not just one drink, but a whole bottle of red, warm oblivion.

FOUR

OH! WHAT A NIGHT

Detectives Kelly and Collins shoot the bull across a battered brown desk in a battered brown room at the police station near Gary's crashpad. It's been a slow, slow day; the phone hasn't jangled out a crime or even a pub brawl.

'How's that harlot murder coming along?' Kelly drawls out the question to Collins who's stifling a yawn. He leans back in the hard chair; the front legs lift off the floor, then sink back slowly as he finds the necessary words in reply 'It's coming along.' He rocks back and forth. 'Fine, just fading away, fading away into the wide blue yonder. No one, and I mean no one, wants it solved. Those whores really get around, you know what I mean?' He winks a languid eye, bloodshot and blue.

'Yeah,' his mate says chewing over the word, his hand intent on doodling a gallows on the blotting pad in front of him. 'Then, what's one pro more or less, especially one past her prime. There's enough new talent to fill her shoes.'

'Or were,' Collins grunts. 'They've all gone to ground, scared that they'll get it too.' He yawns showing a tobacco-stained set of dentures. He's not at all interested in the headquarters' case. After all, what's one murder compared to the crushing boredom pressing down on him? The only thing he doesn't like is that it is keeping the girls from plying their trade openly, and that means less free arse and pin money. God, he thinks, things are really slow in this town – too damn slow. Why, even the dope pushers were co-operating and on first name terms with the members of the drug squad. He sighs. W.A. was like that – small – and everyone got to know everyone else.

'Jesus, I wish something big would happen, say a nice bank job,' dreams Kelly, smiling at the fantasy. He sees his name splashed right across the front sheet in glaring headlines. Yep, a bank job would be just the thing. One with guns. A shootout meant citations for bravery and a promotion taking him right up the ladder to headquarters and the juicy cases. His smile broadens, then collapses: nothing ever happens in this district. He shirks from the grim picture of a future taken up with an occasional breaking and entry, or the punching up of a few drunken boongs. What he needs, he knows, is a big case to take him right to the moon.

'Christ, things are really off,' he groans in disgust and receives a grunt in answer from his mate.

A uniformed cop pokes his head into the room and with a jerk of his head signifying some sort of nut, growls: 'Some bloke to see you. About drugs, I think.'

'Send him in' – anything to break up the warm tedium of the evening, then a big drug bust is news, but it has to be big and they have to get in far ahead of the headline grabbing drug squad: the glamour boys of the force.

They aren't prepared for Ron. The man sidles through the doorway; stops just inside the room, and surveys every inch of the space before committing himself. He vanishes and appears at a spot directly in front of the desk. The two detectives stare up at the Beaufort Street nut. They make a try for his eyes behind the reflecting shades and look away from their own faces. There just might be something here to break their boredom.

'Well, Ronny,' Kelly calls, assuming a rough joviality, his way of humouring the less fortunate, 'what've you got for us this time?'

'Yeah, what've you got?' the tough Collins adds, without interest. This nut is no news to him.

They assume their best steely-hard faces. Ron stands in front of them without a word. Their eyes ricochet off the mirror sunglasses like spent bullets. The man's face begins a slow stop and go around the room. His eyes (it can be deduced from the direction of his nose) rest on the old model typewriter on a sidetable, then on the chipped surface of the desk and finally, after moving across the dusty floorboards and the dirty walls, on the barred and filthy window. The two policemen yawn while this is going on. Faintly amused, they wait for their shift to be over and then to a club for a nice cold bit of the amber, on the house of course.

Finally, out of patience, Collins tries to bring the game to an end. 'We're waiting,' he grunts out, failing to smother another yawn. His mouth gapes and the eagle-eyed alert detective turns into a flabby aging man. 'Come on,' he grates out, seeing his reflection and not liking it.

In reply, Ron leans over the desk, moving the great beak of his nose closer, too close to the men. Not intending to, they recoil a fraction: this nut should be put away where he belongs!

'Well, we're waiting,' Kelly commands. 'Out with it!'

In reply the man slowly reaches into a pocket and pulls out a small, clear plastic tobacco pouch holding about an ounce of dried green herb.

'What's that?' demands Collins.

'There's this place just off William street rented by some wog ...'

'What sort of wog?'

'Indian,' Ron states.

'Oh, a coloured wog, we've come across him before.'

'And,' Ron continues, 'there's about half a dozen Abo bludgers hanging about the place.'

'Yeah, we know about the boongs.'

'Well, the other night,' the man continues to grind out slowly and surely like a cement mixer. 'I went there after midnight and there was this funny smell hanging in the air. You know, a smell like straw burning. And when I came into the room, this Abo girl hid something, but they couldn't put anything over old Ron. No one can do that and get away with it. I kept my eyes open and didn't let on about the smell. Later in the kitchen, I found this.' He pokes out a gnarled finger and gently touches the plastic pouch. 'That's that *mary-anna*, that's what it is.' And the man smiles a smile as if expecting a pat on the back for being a good little, though very old, boy.

Kelly picks up the pouch, weighs it in his hand, opens it with thick fingers and takes out a pinch of the green herb, sniffs it, then tastes it.

'Parsley,' he grunts out contemptuously. 'What'd you bring this stuff to us for? We ain't got a restaurant here. Now take this stuff and get out before you find out what sort of place this is.'

He flings the bag at Ron. The herb sprays out over the man's hat and sunglasses.

'But, but,' the Beaufort Street nut protests, trying to retrieve something from the situation. 'This ain't all. They got two little girls living there. Real young ones, not a day over fourteen, just ripe for the picking.' He leers. 'You know what those boongs and wogs are like? You get me! You better keep an eye on that place.' He leers again to make sure the two detectives get his meaning. 'They don't trust me in there; they know I'm on your side, the side of law and order. You know, I've been in the nut house. It was for my own good; now, I'm cured, but I've seen those wogs and know what they're like. Then, there's that boong, Greg, a real mean bastard. He's been in for bashing blokes. You know that! One of these days if you don't watch him he'll kill someone, could even be me, and what'll happen then?'

Most likely promotion for bringing in a murderer, Kelly thinks. He jerks a thumb towards the doorway and growls: 'Get!'

Ron's face, as much as can be seen, appears to turn cunning, the expression is fox-like, and he wheedles: 'See, I came right over here with this info. I keep my eyes open, I do; and if I see anything crooked I come right on over and tell you blokes. I'm worth something I am, and we're all Aussies here, ain't we? so how about twenty cents for a cup of coffee. Just twenty cents, that's all. It's not asking for much.'

Collins ominously heaves himself to his feet and takes a step towards the nut. In an instant the man dematerialises. The detective falls back into his chair. 'Think there's anything in it?' he asks Kelly.

'Maybe, maybe, what say we check out our contact in the area. If there's any young girls in that place we can raid it.' He looks at the wall clock. 'Too late for anything tonight. End of the shift coming up. How about getting down to that new Mocambo joint and have a look at those topless barmaids they have. Even dance hostesses there; that might mean a tumble.'

'It'll mean at least a jug or two of beer,' his mate agrees, getting to his feet with more enthusiasm than he's shown all evening. He glances down out of the window and is startled to find Ron glinting up at him. Twin lights reflect off the nut's sunglasses. 'God, that loony, he'll go for a row one of these days, mark me.'

'Mad as a hatter for sure,' Kelly grunts.

Meanwhile down in the street the Beaufort Street nut shakes his fist up at the lighted window and snarls curses at the pigs. He'll get them one day. He'll make a bomb and blow all the cops off the face of the earth. What do they know of *mary-anna*; and not even two bob for a cup of coffee. He rubs his hat to get rid of the bits of parsley, passes a grubby handkerchief over his lenses and snarls: 'Fuck all sons of bitches!' Then he turns and glides off through the night.

He reaches a litter bin, stops, and begins to sort through the rubbish of humanity, heaving out old newspapers and paperbags filled with fruit skins. He scatters the litter about the bin – almost to the bottom and not a damned thing!

A car leaves the curb and floods the bin and the shabby apparition with daylight. It whizzes past and Ron makes out the heads of the two detectives.

He flings a plastic bottle after the tail lights. The container bounces flatly, then lies inertly in the middle of the street. Ron returns to the bin and strikes paydirt: a pair of woman's panties. With relish he sinks the great horn of his nose into the material and sniffs deeply and long. He holds them up to the light, waves them triumphantly in the air, then stuffs them beneath his shirt where they nestle against his grey chest hairs. The man dives into the bin again, right to the very bottom to haul out a brown paper bag. He rips it open and gloats over the contents. At last he's found his supper. Satisfied, Ron chuckles and slinks off munching on the stale sandwiches – made with loving care for some son of a bitch by some bitch. How he hates them – all of them! One day he'll get even.

II

Tom's need makes it easy for him to evade the others and reach the hotel bar. His second dole cheque (obtained under an assumed name) has arrived just that morning or noon or night-he isn't exactly sure of the time, but he found it in his pocket, and now he has the money to drink his blues away. In quick succession he downs four pots, then dawdles over a fifth. The glow of alcohol permeates his body and he smiles slowly and peacefully as his narrow restless eyes flicker around the bar. For once he feels a certain security – he's out of his territory and among the middle class who can't relate to things different from themselves. In his clean clothing, Tom sits amongst the mass-suited and is blissfully alone. His smile widens into an Abo grin of contentment. One advantage of being constantly drunk is that it doesn't take much to get a hit.

But his grin reaches out to the broad man sitting next to him – who turns his face fully towards Tom and says: 'How you going?'

Tom replies, letting words on the weather flow from him. It's his way, when he's on the grog. A beer's offered and accepted. The barman swishes down to them and gracefully places the large glass in front of Tom.

'He's more than a little gay,' Tom says matter of factly. He indicates the barman with a jerk of his head. The man, blonde and blue-eyed, slim and clean, neat and well-kept, succeeds in being as attractive as a woman.

'Yeah,' the man beside him replies, 'he's my wife. I live with him.' Tom starts and focuses on the man, muscular and short, a working class hero in jeans and sweat shirt; clean and neat, pink and bulging with muscles. 'Yeah,' the Nungar mumbles. Like they say one never knows, or cares to know. 'He's nice looking,' he adds as an after-thought.

'Yep, he is,' the man says, 'and can he cook. Only thing, he's a little jealous, then so am I for that matter.'

Tom senses that he's getting into some sort of game, a game he doesn't want to play. This happens to him all the time and he doesn't like it. Just look at Alan and the bank business and Sue and that jail back east. Things just happen to him. He considers the subject at the bottom of his beer glass. Life or rather his life is too mixed up a mess for him to try and make sense out of it. God, why doesn't he take off up north and get away from all the craziness? In the desert with the vast flatness eroding away the horizon, he could try and get his mind together. He downs his sixth beer in one swallow, and gives a fatalistic shrug – he'll have another, then go to Obelia's. More craziness; he watches the barman swish down to him. More craziness!

'Another one?'

'Yah,' Tom replies, looking away, sensing the violence in the man beside him. The Nungar isn't interested in anything except adding further to his stone and other trips don't move him, or do they? He doesn't care enough to think it out.

The barman returns with the beer, puts it down and while taking up the money, suddenly demands: 'Where's Jack?'

'Jack?' The man who had been beside him is there no longer. 'Hope he doesn't get into another blue,' the barman says, wrinkling his smooth brow.

'Why?' Tom questions. 'Looks like he can take care of himself.'

'That's the trouble. I just hope that one of these days he gets his head punched in. It'll teach him a lesson.'

'It might,' the Nungar half agrees, unable to summon up an interest in Jack's constant brawling. He downs his beer, smiling more and more broadly as his mind numbs. 'Want me to go and check?' he suddenly asks the barman in a swift surge of comradeship. 'He might need someone to protect his back' – but the man's moving away and doesn't hear him. Tom dismisses the idea and stares down into his empty beer glass. Does he want another, or doesn't he?

A bloke moves to his side, a ruddy Irish type, short and energetic, a person who should have a jaunty hat cocked to one side of his fresh, round face.

'Where're you from, not from these parts, are you?' the lad jerks out in assumed friendliness.

'Over the hills and from far away,' Tom replies, grinning.

'The east?' the lad persists.

'The east, among other places,' Tom echoes with the same grin.

'Sydney?'

'No, Melbourne.'

'Have you tried the local special?' the larrikin says with an expression he thinks is one of letting a stranger into a real good local drink.

Tom, a constant victim of gags, lets himself go along, asking tiredly: 'No, what is it?'

'The Wally Wombat,' the larrikin seems to answer, though the Nungar misses the words. 'Try it, mate, guaranteed to blow your head off your shoulders.'

Tom appears to consider before making a positive decision: 'How much will it set me back?'

'Only a dollar fifty.'

'Why not?'

'It'll really get you pissed,' the lad shouts into Tom's passiveness.

'Yeah,' the Nungar seems to agree, and counts out his money in coins. He's willing to try anything for that final drink, including this mixture of bottle dregs, guaranteed to blast him into drunkenness.

The larrikin winks at the barmaid who's just replaced the gay. She strolls down to them.

'Give the man a Wally Wombat.'

Tom catches the grin cracking her makeup. He lights a cigarette. The drink's put in front of him; he tastes it, and declares that there's too much orange; but the joke's over.

The lad, after wishing Tom the best of luck, goes off with a swagger. The Nungar downs the drink and feels his head swirl: a joke isn't a joke when you can get off on it. With a drunken grin plastered across his face, he staggers out into the street where he stands waiting for the night to steady about him. The cool evening breeze, somewhat belatedly, has arrived and he lets it caress his skin.

Then someone charges past him almost knocking him off his feet. The Nungar turns and sees the butch camp, in a flaming rage, tearing off along a lane. The lad's the object of his charge. Tom walks after him and passes just as Jack lets go a terrific kick which sends the larrikin sprawling. The lad tries to get to his feet, only to meet a descending fist which rips blood from his nose.

'That'll teach you to touch my car, you fucking thief,' Jack snarls. The larrikin makes it to his feet and hares it down a dark alley.

Jack rushes after him. Tom crosses the street, lurching towards Obelia's. There, it's at least peaceful.

III

Obelia's Coffee Lounge is a huge gloomy basement, a refuge of a sort for the odd bods and freaks of Perth. It's owned and run by a black-bearded Jew who Tom doesn't like because he once refused him a glass of water. The Jew isn't there and Tom goes to the counter and nods at the serving girl. The owner doesn't pay his help much and there's a rapid turnover of staff as travellers desperate for money settle in for a day or two, then move on.

'A coffee,' he requests, looking into the girl's eyes. They're easy to look into, and they stare back confidently.

'A coffee, it is,' she smiles, 'black?' He catches a Yankee accent and grins as he imagines the CIA after Alan and his mob.

He passes over a dollar when she puts the cup in front of him. She hands him the change; their hands touch.

'Been here long?' Tom asks, slowly withdrawing his hand. Drunk, he is often friendly.

'A week.' She flashes her teeth which are bright and very white.

'And what do you think of Perth?'

'It's a pretty little city, though I haven't seen much of it yet.'

'Might show you around, that is if you want to see more of it.' Tom says, stumbling over his words. He doesn't like offering any of his time.

'Sure, that'll be fine,' the girl answers with an overbright smile which he finds a little phony – or at least, cultivated.

'See you in a while,' he grins, taking up his coffee and glancing around for Alan and Sue.

He finds them sitting at a small table holding a horizontal video tube and stands watching them play telly tennis. Both are intent on the game and don't notice him. Alan twists a knob which causes a small rectangular patch of light to appear to move back and forth across the board in front of him. Sue manipulates a similar racquet. She sends the ball, a small dot of light, towards Alan's side of the board. He catches it on his racquet and glances it off a sidewall. Sue returns it. He contacts the dot with his rectangle of light and it drifts lazily towards the girl. She over-reacts. The glowing dot moves past her bat and blinks out. The board bleeps once and the score flashes on: 11-10. Alan's the victor. The racquets disappear; the board returns to neutral, and the ball blips from side to side waiting to be engaged in play when twenty cents is fed in.

'Want a game, Tom?' Alan asks, obviously pleased at winning. 'You can play Sue first and get your hand in.'

Tom shakes his head. He isn't into games and moreover his hands are too shaky.

Alan flashes a glance from Tom to Sue, then suddenly leaps to his feet. 'I'm off.' He flashes a grin. 'Got to see a friend, might be back later.' And before they realise it, he's scooting away.

'That kid sure has energy,' Tom says in admiration. His knees feel ready to give and he slumps into a chair.

Sue looks him over, then walks off to a corner table. He gets up and follows her with his cup of coffee and offers her a sip. The girl takes it up, tastes it, then puts it back on the table. 'You've been drinking again,' she accuses him.

'So what,' Tom replies, anger flaring in his mind. 'So bloody what,' he grinds out. 'I like to drink.' He mutters, 'It's my life.' Why does this girl always get through his defences? 'Anyway,' he tries for an attack, 'why don't we get it off, then I might forget the grog?'

'Don't make me laugh, you're too chicken to face life without a crutch.'

'Am I?' he slurs out, faking more than feeling and sliding into an old defensive pattern. 'You know, many a man has been saved by a woman.'

'Don't give me any of that crap,' Sue replies savagely. 'You turn me off, that you do. Who wants a man without any guts?'

'Gutless,' Tom agrees, trying for a grin and failing: it's true, he is gutless!

'You know, every time we meet, it's the same old tale,' the girl hits out. 'You just don't try.' She turns to sweet reason: 'Why don't you pull yourself together and help yourself and us? You know how Alan likes you, you're his uncle, and we're friends, comrades that we are, and everyone of us has to be strong.'

'O.K. we're friends,' Tom attempts a sneer; 'but first we get it off, then after we'll act the solidarity thing.'

The girl rolls her eyes heavenwards and Tom feels his anger growing. 'You're waiting for that white bloke, ain't you?' he accuses her.

'What if I am? He's my boyfriend,' the girl retorts.

'Nothing much, only seeing we're into the brothers and sisters thing, how come you're screwing around with the enemy? He ain't no citizen of Nungarland.'

'Oh, come off it! I'm sick and tired of this stuff you put out. You lay all this, this shit on me, and you don't mean any of it – it's just a game to you. You're not interested in me or even in Alan. All you want is grog and if you ain't got that, you're finished. Why don't you just get lost!'

'It ain't exactly like that at all,' Tom weakly protests, while wondering what exactly it is like. 'It could be more; must be more – is more,' he protests, trying to put sincerity into his voice. He can't make it and gives a sudden shrill laugh: 'What does it all matter, anyway?'

'It matters,' replies Sue, feeling pity for him. He seems such a lost little boy. 'It matters,' she says again. 'You know Alan's planning this thing, and you're a part of it. Use your brain, help him and all of us.' The girl leans forward and touches his shoulder, trying to instil confidence into him.

'Yeah, yeah,' Tom replies, looking into her sincere face and not liking such a display of real emotion. 'Yeah, yeah,' he repeats, desperately. 'I don't know what's going to happen. All I know is that it scares me. Alan's just a kid and ready for anything; but I'm sick of hell!' He smiles sickly, gives a hacking cough, then gets up: he needs another drink – for confidence, for numbness!

The girl watches his retreating back. She feels a terrible pity for him, but knows that he must learn, grow strong or go under as so many of her people have gone under. She hates this weakness as she hates drunkenness. If only he wasn't so negative, so much a bum and able to accept being a bum. She watches his back pass through the door and catches the appearance of Ron. Next moment, he is at her table. She tries to push a smile past his mirror shades, and watches it fade away.

Ron stands for an over long moment, his eyes seeking into the darkest corners of the basement. He catches sight of the proprietor and snarls something under his breath – then, he's sitting in the chair opposite Sue, draining the remains of Tom's coffee.

'Seen Alan?' Ron jerks out.

'He left a couple of minutes ago,' the girl replies, darting a quick glance at the mirrors. She suppresses a shudder: is he as harmless as Alan says?

'You know,' Ron rumbles deep down in this throat, 'Alan's a fine kid, one of the best. I think the world of him. He and I are like this.' He pokes up two grubby fingers and brings them together. 'I taught him a lot, that's why he doesn't turn me away as he does the others. I don't like that wog, Gary, that Greg – any of them! They ain't got anything upstairs, not like Alan. No, Alan's a good mate of mine, that he is – but the others, one day I'll get them. Where's Alan?' he jerks out at the frightened girl, enjoying her fright, feeding on it.

'You know,' he drools out, 'they put me in the loony bin for a lot of years, and for something I didn't do. No, I never touched that lying slut. They're all like that. I know what they say about me. All except Alan. He's a mate, he is. Where is he now?'

'He went off to see a friend,' Sue manages to say. Even if she knew where he'd gone, she wouldn't tell this creep.

'He takes drugs!' the man declares.

'Never,' Sue rises in defence of Alan.

'Not like Tom and Greg,' Ron says, angling for information.

'Tom's on the grog. No one I know takes any of those drugs.'

'Well, what about the funny smell that's around in Gary's place?' the man insinuates.

'Incense, Gary's Indian and all Indians like that stuff.'

'Yeah, they're funny, those wogs,' Ron agrees, then switches the subject. 'And what about those funny pictures on the walls?' he jerks out, following it up with an attempt at a laugh.

The girl is over her fright and replies as Alan would: 'It's election time and we support Labor. It's the best government Australia's ever had.'

'Never done anything for me,' Ron sneers. 'Those bastards are only good to themselves.' He veers back to Alan. 'Not like Alan, he's good to me, he is. You know what he's trying to do? He helping me to get the shit out of my head. They put me in the loony bin and fucked me up real good. And they keep fucking me up,' the man hisses, making the girl jerk back as if from a venomous snake. Ron sucks in the effect and leans closer to her, moving his face from side to side so that light glints off and on his sunglasses. 'You know, Janet, the girl who's fond of me, told me to meet her here tonight. But she isn't here. Been having me on, just like the rest of the tarts,' he growls out; 'just like the rest of them. They take all you've got, then throw you out, just like the slut that had me sent up.' He stops, panting, spittle flows to the corners of his mouth. He pulls the brim of his hat down until it touches the tops of his sunglasses, then grinds out his obsession: 'But she's a nice one, looks almost sixteen, just like I like them. You know she really plays with me. She comes into the room when I visit her in one of those sheer nightgown things and her tits poke out of the top. She lets me look as long as I want to. Then she sits with her legs apart, giving me an eyeful. I might be going on fifty, but I can still go all night-you know what I mean! Why just today, I went to her house and she let me in. She's good that way, and I can always get a bite to eat there. Well, you know what she did this time? She took off her panties and gave them to me.' Ron fumbles under his trenchcoat and shirt and pulls out a pair of panties and waves them at the frightened girl. He quickly hides them again.

The girl is trembling; wants to escape, but feels glued to her chair. Her eyes flick about the dark basement. Tom appears at the door. She prays for him to come over. He doesn't; and the vile man rubs her thigh as he whispers obscenities into her ear. The whispers pierce through her as she wills Tom to come to her rescue.

The Nungar doesn't. He sees a pimply faced youth slouched in a chair in the darkest corner of the basement and goes to him.

'Man, I've got just the thing for you,' the youth smirks up at him.

Tom flops into a chair and the youth falls into a whisper of false intensity: 'Man, it's a bargain. Acid tabs, full moons, five dollars a trip – and these are good. The real stuff, no bullshit! I know acid, I've tried them all: Californian sunset, starlight and moonbright, and this is the very best. It's easy to get ripped off, but this is fair dinkum, the real McCoy.'

'Arrh, come on,' Tom slurs a snarl. 'I've been east where the good stuff is. I remember that grass you sold me, not to mention the hash oil.'

'No man, this is it, and only five dollars a tab. You just take it and you'll be flying. It's the very best, man!'

Tom stares away, and sees Ron sitting with Sue. He knows the man and can guess what the girl is being subjected to. He smiles: it'll teach her a thing or two. He grins across at the pusher. 'I'm a little low at present, how about two for five, and then, if they're as good as you say they are, I'll give you the rest the next time I see you?'

'I've got to think about it,' the pimply faced youth replies, pretending to think by screwing up his face.

'You know me,' Tom adds, 'and if they're as good as you say, I'll give you a dollar extra.'

'Yeah, man, yeah,' the dealer nods. 'Well, just for you, we know each other, but don't let on to anyone else, or they'll want them for two and a half. It'd ruin my business.'

The Nungar fiddles around in his pocket, finds a five and flips it across the table. The pusher goes into an elaborate pantomime of secrecy. Trying to be the magician, he winks and there in front of Tom lies a small square of folded tinfoil. Disdaining the dramatics, he opens it and inspects the two round circles of blotting paper. 'Right on,' he grins and, refolding the square, leaves the table with a stagger.

The fast talking Ron instantly becomes aware of the man coming in their direction. His stream of profanity dries up in midspurt; one moment he's sitting at the table, the next nowhere in sight.

'Well, well, getting it off with old Ron,' Tom drawls, almost falling into a chair. 'What'd he want? I suppose the same old crap. How's Janet going? She still giving him the old run around? I've listened to that guy so many times I know his whole rap.'

Sue gulps for air and whispers in a thin little girl's voice: 'Tom, he's crazy, he's sick. God, I'm glad you came. He gives me the willies. I thought I'd heard everything, until I heard that guy.'

'Yeah,' Tom says, feeling glad that the girl's glad to have him at her side. 'But he's harmless as they come; wouldn't hurt a fly – all words. You know, he spent seventeen years in the nut house.'

'And no wonder,' Sue whimpers. 'He kept on saying these awful things. How he was going to cut people up and, you know, things like digging up bodies in the cemetery. He said he wanted to get a job in the morgue so that he could – I just can't say it.'

'I know, I know,' Tom whispers, patting her arm. 'Take no notice, just say "Yes, Ron," now and again and he'll be satisfied. Hey, to get your mind off things, how about coming on a trip with me, I've got some acid.'

'You mean L.S.D.,' the girl exclaims, quickly getting over the nut. 'You don't take that poison, do you Tom? It's just too much! I don't like your drinking, but I can accept that if you try to give it up; but this other stuff, that I can't. Why do you want to destroy yourself? Leave it alone. Listen to Alan. He's tried these things, and doesn't like them.'

'Alan, Alan, that's all I hear these days,' Tom says petulantly. 'What does he know about anything? He's all wet behind the ears. I do what I want!'

'Well, don't come whining to me,' Sue snaps. 'I've had it up to here!'

In answer, Tom squeezes her breast.

'Hurry up and you can catch up with that friend of yours,' Sue says angrily. 'You're two of a kind!'

'Oh, fuck you,' Tom snaps, and gets up with a lurch, then meanders to the counter.

Sue feels sorry for him, but then her boyfriend comes to the table and she feels happy to be with someone steady and sane.

IV

Tom sits with the American girl, Sherri: lilywhite, blonde and beautiful, the American dream slightly askew with a dumpy figure; but the intensity of emotion she brings to an ordinary conversation makes up for it. The Nungar feels that he's found a pair of sympathetic eyes and ears and switches to a spiel of how the blacks are treated in Western Australia. Sympathetically, the girl contrasts the position of the American Indians, and agrees that the world, indeed, does need changing for the better. Then Tom, feeling that he has made a score, mentions acid, and the girl's all aglow to try it and contrast it. It's been simply months since she's had a trip.

'Where did you drop it?' a softer Tom asks.

'Honolulu, right on the beach. They sure do have nice beaches there.'

'We could go to a beach and drop this,' Tom suggests.

'Sure, would be real neat,' Sherri replies, flashing her perfect teeth.

'What sort of acid is it? Microdots, clearpanel?'

'No full moons,' the man replies, bringing out the folded square of tinfoil and showing her the two circles of blotting paper. 'If we hurry we can catch the last bus to Cottesloe. It's nice and quiet there.'

'Let's go, man,' Sherri says, leaping up and hurrying him along and out the door.

FIVE

SANDAWARA GOES TO WAR

The old man sitting bent over his fire roams far in his dreamland – through the good times to the bad in exile. Black, lost and powerless, there are few opportunities to buy the illegal bottled warmth he needs. But Jacky Jacky is picturesque with his rugged face and flowing grey beard, and if he shows his man scars he becomes even more of an asset. Some white men want to preserve or display the ways of the blacks. It is their way of atoning for the guilt they feel and also a sign of showing they belong to the country – but the old ways have been almost totally wiped out: few know the sacred dances and fewer will display them before the aliens. Jacky Jacky allows himself to be bought; allows himself with some others to be collected together to stage a makeshift corroboree. In front of a group of chatting foreigners, he slouches waiting to display his culture. He feels totally alienated: an actor, a performer – a monkey pantomiming for bananas. An ape, he postures. Hair clad in a red bandana, face masked in white ash, coward's wounds slashed with a warrior's scorn, he stands waiting for the show to start. But Jacky Jacky's got a thirst to satisfy and knows that a few tired jigs'll bring in enough brass for a dozen bottles of sweet wine and that is all he wants. The Law slumbers deep within his heart protected from the poisonous blanket of red liquor.

Another like himself drones out a sacred song turned blasphemous; others like himself join in, hands beating the flat earth. Pum, pum, a passive rhythm without life – or hope. Jacky Jacky hesitates, his dark brown body flabby and as soft as flour. He feels a very faint breeze of freedom touching his skin. So gentle, so faint that it can be pushed aside and ignored. His shabby white man's clothing has been discarded – but it still imprisons his heart. He feels a slave and wishes he didn't care. Once (why should he remember?), the real Law ruled strong; once (is it true?), he stood the Law-holder – and now? ... The white men sit to one side in the shade watching and smiling at the antics of the blacks. The song becomes captured by laughter and ends. The performers feel their isolation and shame. Even a white woman stares – at the sacred dances hidden and secret from all females. Now, no more! What had they done to separate themselves from their ancestors; what enormous crime had they committed to offend the Lawgivers and to bring on such a terrible punishment? Guilty under his own Law, Jacky Jacky moves to do his dance before the aliens.

Another song begins: a song of Sandawara, the last of the warriors to fight-and die! The men begin, their voices low and tame, then rise, hating and exultant. The spirit of Sandawara moves them. Again in the eternal time the police ride out to die and the freedom fighter stands triumphant, holding high the kidney of his enemy.

With a wild shout Noorak leaps from Jacky Jacky and springs high into the sky. His old body is forgotten; strength flows through him; he feels as if the old times have returned. Around him, the voices chant out the legend, each word a grunt of acknowledgement. The men swarm to defend their earth and the Law holds firm – as firm as Sandawara.

Noorak leaps high to land with a widespread, earth-shaking jar. He struts two steps, lordly and wise – powerful! His feet stamp in time to the singing, in time to the surging rhythm. Sandawara is in command. The hopes of the people rise and fill their land. Warriors clasp their long war spears, shout with righteous anger and glow with hope – glorious hope. They charge out to gain their own. Once again, their earth their earth; their Law, the only law. At the head of his people Sandawara is out against the invader.

He stamps about the fire, his knees high, his feet hammering at the earth – to subdue it, to reclaim it as his own. His first ancestors passed across this land, leaving it intact but known. Each tree, each bush, each animal, the waterholes and soaks were named and formed into a loving oneness of people and earth. No one raped and no one pillaged; love formed the bond and the Law held firm each and every particle until – the singing rises to a higher pitch. Three white outlaws die. The tempo quickens as Sandawara hunts down the police. Noorak runs and leaps, sways backwards and forwards in mortal combat with a many handed demon. The rhythm hastens and begins to slow, keeping pace with the battle. The warrior falls away in momentary defeat, then rises up to another victory. Sandawara calls upon his people; Sandawara captures guns – and among the bored onlookers an outlaw crushes his cigarette butt into the alien earth with a boot heel as hard as steel and gets to his feet.

Jacky Jacky falls to the ground; the singing goes ragged, and the rhythm clicks out disjointedly. The white man stalks off into the sunset. The Law is lost as Sandawara is lost. Jacky Jacky worn out by his vision and the struggle lifts his body to its feet. The singers trail off, the rhythm falters and stops as the rest of the white audience moves away. Some shake their heads sadly at the loss of a culture. The glorious days are gone and Jacky Jacky feels the coldness of the universe and wants only the warmth of wine.

The old man sits alone at the fire, living again his old memories, feeling again the old pain in his heart.

Then hope glides up to him with a bottle of sweet wine to soothe his hurt. Thankfully he sucks at the bottle, letting the warmth flow through his old body. 'Tell me of Sandawara,' Alan coaxes, 'tell me of Sandawara.' His large dark eyes reach out to the elder. 'Yes, Sandawara,' the old man's voice murmurs, falling and rising in the night as Sandawara rises and falls in the night of his earth.

II

Sandawara stands a little apart from the others. Deep-chested and long-legged he reclaims his earth. It is his own and beyond and before. He raises an arm horizontally and sweeps it across the waiting men. His deepset eyes flash as he commands: 'Get the guns and all the bullets there are. Get the food. Pile it on the verandah, there!' His arm lowers and his clenched fist hits out. 'And watch those who aren't with us. Don't let any get away to carry tales to the police.'

Instantly, without a murmur, he is obeyed – even by Ellewara who considers himself the destined leader, and is the very best of the many to take up spears against the white invader; but he lacks vision and now, confronted by the ex-police boy, finds himself a follower. And he, the proud Ellewara, the killer of more than one white man, doesn't like it. His fierce eyes glare at the leader towering before him, rifle in hand. He hates his position, but knows he must follow. For, Sandawara knows the ways of the foe; knows the use of guns; knows how to command and be obeyed. The warrior glares and can do nothing. He stares at Captain, the loyal second-in-command, lounging with his hand loosely around the butt of his revolver and turns away. Sandawara is the leader – until death and beyond when he'll live in the songs of his people. Now he stands there watching the prisoners being freed.

Word will spread out from camp to camp and warriors will feel a stirring in their hearts of battles to be fought and won. Clutching their serrated war spears, once deadly but now useless, they will lope across the earth to him.

All the land moves, whirling like a cyclone, and the eye of the storm is this man, Sandawara, who sits apart from the others, his mind weighing the odds and thinking only of the final victory. One way to go and that is forward until his people regain their own for ever. Sunk in thought, he sits apart from the others and carefully cleans the rifle he has captured from the policeman. This gun, a Winchester, he feels to be part of his magic, and he will guard it as he does his life. Caressing the warm metal of his striking arm, exulting in the touch of a fine weapon, he still knows that it needs more than one repeating rifle to free his earth. More and more must be collected, and his men must be trained to use them. But where is he to get the guns and how long will it take to train his men? He sighs and lies down to rest, clasping his rifle to his chest as he sinks into the dreamland and strikes out through mist towards a future. Deep within his dream a plan is given to him. He learns how to get rifles and quickly.

Dawn breaks with a whoop from the fierce Ellewara, vibrant as the newly born sun, but unable to see beyond the sunset, the next waterhole and gulp of water – so unlike Sandawara who greets the day with a sigh. He stares at his mob squatting about the fires and remembers the plan. Given in vision, he knows it is the way.

He looks at his fierce followers. Brave and hardy, those who have trudged for miles choking on a chain are free and ready to defend their freedom. Ready, yes, but without the guns necessary for success.

Sandawara turns his eyes on Ellewara, the impetuous and dangerous one who cannot resist playing the leader. 'We'll kill every policeman in our land,' he roars out, 'and every white man – one by one!' The warriors roar back as he shakes his newly acquired shotgun. 'The hill tribes are for us and the plains folk are at our side.' But Sandawara knows the man can hardly fire his gun let alone hit the target.

Ellewara, the born demagogue, shouts and boasts though without the necessary skill to win through. His voice, his gestures, his gleaming eyes sway all to his side – all but Sandawara sitting alone and apart. Ellewara sees him and holding the men in the palm of his strong hand tries for the leader. He begins to talk of semi-sacred things:

'In this land, up in the hills,' he begins, his long arm moving the heads of the men to the rugged mountains squatting on the horizon, 'there are many caves. Once, a long time ago, one such deep and dark cave was the home of man-eating dingoes. It was a place like that Derby town.' He waits for the connection to be made. 'Every day those beasts would go out after us, hunting us down just like the police do. When they caught any of us, be it man, woman, or little child, they would drag them back to their cave. There, they made a dinner of them.' The man smacks his lips and the audience starts.

Ellewara hesitates, too long, as he looks towards Sandawara. With sullen lips and lowered brows, the leader is intent on examining each cartridge before pushing it into a loop in the cartridge belt. Ellewara looks. He knows Sandawara has a way with guns. He knows that it is with weapons, not words, that victory can be won and the white man driven away.

Ellewara's voice strives to reach Sandawara, he continues: 'A Willy-wagtail man, Jitta-jitta wanted to free his people from the menace. He formed a plan of waiting at the mouth of the cave and of killing the dingoes one by one as they emerged. To do this he needed helpers and tried to get the men of his people to follow him. They were afraid and he had to give them courage. Taking a heavy club he went to the cave and hid near the entrance. A huge dingo came trotting out. He hit out at the animal and struck it dead without a sound to give him away.' Ellewara mimes the action and the men participate in the death of the dingo.

Sandawara glances up at the warrior prancing about with his almost useless gun held high like a spear. He listens to him. 'Then Jitta-jitta took up the body of the animal and lugged it back to camp. All the people flocked around to marvel at the warrior. The men gained courage and followed the Willy-wagtail man back to the cave. They hid and when the dingoes come out, they killed them one by one – and that's how we'll fix the white men,' he cries. 'We'll go to the river, to that white man Lukin's place. We'll burn him out, we'll eat his kidney – now!' He leaps about in a frenzy and the mob spring up to join him – all except Sandawara calmly preparing his weapon.

The leader gets to his feet, buckling the cartridge belt about his waist. Casually he examines his rifle and jacks a shell into the breech, then he strides towards the excited men. He stops and waits silently. His eyes flicker like lightning and the stamping and shouting of the warriors cease. He watches their chests heaving and their eyes glaring. Good men all ready to follow, and too valuable to let Ellewara throw away in foolhardy schemes. They wait for him to speak and he knows what to say.

Sandawara speaks: 'We leave Lukin and his place alone. He's useless to us. We need guns and more guns.' He smiles at Ellewara. 'And we must have time to learn how to use those guns. Soon, too soon, the police will ride out. We must be ready for them. Ellewara has just outlined his plans for us,' he says quietly, 'but in my country there is another story about dingoes. Binurrineri, the Warmala, was a devilman who loved to eat human flesh. All men were game to him. He came from the east where the white men dwell and with him ran a pack of devil dingoes. They had eyes of fire, bright white strong teeth and claws as sharp as eagle's talons. A brave man could not kill them. It needed more than bravery, for they were evil and spears glanced from their skins. More and more people were caught and the elders came together to find a way to rid themselves of the evil. They decided to call on the men of power. The powermen with their power tools stalked Binurrineri. At last, they came face to face with him and were surprised when he greeted them and invited them to his camp. Though suspecting a trap, they went with the devilman for they were unafraid with their weapons of power. At the camp, they sat down. Instantly, the devil dingoes sprang out from ambush and leapt at their throats. But the mapans, shamans, had strong magic and were unafraid. The animals found their fangs gnashing on solid stone. The powermen had formed shields to protect themselves from the onslaught. They could not be hurt and they had the weapons to destroy the demon-man and his devil pack. I tell you this, because it is not courage alone that will win the day but strong weapons in the hands of strong men. We need guns and more guns. Only then can we meet the devil white man on his own ground and completely destroy him. There is no other way.'

Sandawara pauses and to the men it seems that the whole earth waits for him to continue.

'There are three other white men. We attack them, kill them, take their cattle and loot their waggon. We do this in the same way as Ellewara has described. We'll ambush those dingoes.'

He stops, letting the warriors see the vision he has found in his dream.

One by one, their faces light up. A masterstroke. They all know that for weeks three white men – Burke, Gibbs and Edgar – have been marching towards the King Leopold range to conquer more land and dispossess more people. They travel with cattle, spare horses, stockboys and a bullock waggon laden with a year's supplies.

'We wipe out these invaders,' concludes Sandawara in a low voice which reaches beyond the cluster of warriors, 'take their guns and all that they have. On the waggon will be rifles and bullets, axes, knives, iron and food. We'll take the horses and let those who are not fighters drive the cattle into the hills to feed our people, and then ...'

'We go and wipe out old Lukin,' shouts Ellewara.

His shout shatters against a 'No' from Sandawara.

'No,' he repeats. 'By the time we've finished with them, a police patrol'll be riding fast from Derby. I know,' the former tracker says, 'for we have killed one of them and that they do not like. Even now that patrol might be saddling up. Soon it'll ride out. When we finish the three, it'll be near Lukin's place and he'll join them.'

Again he pauses, his eyes roaming from tense face to tense face. His soft voice reaches out like a caress. 'They'll ride on to where the waggon is. They'll find the dead men and stop. Our warriors will be hidden around the place.' His voice rises to a whip lash: 'We'll wipe out all of those dingoes!'

The men shout and stamp their feet. Ellewara scowls for a long moment, then joins in the shouting. Sandawara lifts a hand and they go silent. Now he speaks harshly, intently, passionately: 'When those policemen are dead, we'll have their guns and bullets – enough guns and bullets for our needs. So many of our people will be armed that never again shall the white man dare to walk our earth. We'll wipe out the cattle stations, then that evil town of Derby. We'll chase them far away and be free. Our earth will again be our earth; our Law again our law, and then our ways shall endure!'

The men leap and rattle their weapons. Already they feel themselves free from the hated invader – but Sandawara frowns ...

III

The land shouts with the heat and rumours that the people have risen to fight. The cattle drift slowly across the plain like an army. The herd is commanded by Burke and Gibbs aided by the stockboys, Georgy and Nigger. A few miles behind the herd rolls the battle waggon heavy and inert in its cloud of dust. The white man, Edgar, rides his grey horse a little ahead of the toiling team, guided by the tame black, Sambo.

Towards noon the thirsty cattle invade the gorge country and charge towards the Wandjina waterhole. Surrounded by high sandstone cliffs, the five kilometre stretch of water rests in peace amid tangled clumps of trees, creepers and grass. Wildfowl flee, squawking as the lumbering beasts bawl their way over the banks and thud down to pollute the pool.

Frank Burke, the grizzled oldtimer, rides slowly around the drove. He stops next to his mate, Billy Gibbs, a young pink Englishman. The old man fills his pipe and grunts: 'Everything's quiet.'

'Looks like it,' the young man agrees. Nothing has happened on the march to jar his boredom.

The two guards separate and circle away. Something makes Burke glance towards a cliff face. Startled he glimpses a rifle barrel pointing at his face. Behind the muzzle squints a black face: Sandawara! The old man slowly inches his hand to the revolver at his waist. He knows blacks can't handle guns. He'll bring the bugger down for sure.

The defenders of the waterhole open fire. The blast of the rifle almost knocks Burke from his horse. The crack tears from rocky wall to rocky wall. The man's mount bounds off into the undergrowth, the corpse still in the saddle – but not for long. Ellewara jumps up from behind a pile of rocks and lets fly. Boom, the double blast of a shotgun rips the body apart. The terrified horse bolts, dragging a mangled mass behind it.

Gibb's boredom flees as fear for his life enters. He tries to charge his way out of the trap. He manages to let off a shot, then another – and causes the cattle to stampede. They mill and bawl and block his escape. Sandawara coolly aims and fires. The man lurches in the saddle. Another well-placed shot and Gibbs tumbles to the ground – dead! The stockboys manage to make it to the scrub. They hide among the trees and watch as Sandawara's men rush into the open. A shout leaps up from the side of the pool. The terror-stricken stockboy, Georgy, is discovered hiding behind a tree. Quickly he is secured by Lillewara and brought before the leader of the freedom fighters. His cool derisive eyes mock the traitor. Sandawara states softly: 'You work for the white man!' Georgy nods, fear holds his tongue.

'You work no more for the white man. Join us.!'

The man's teeth began to chatter.

'You work no more for the white man,' commands Sandawara.

Georgy cannot answer.

Sandawara levels his rifle. 'Join us?' he quietly asks again.

The man stands trembling in silence.

The leader lowers his gun. He has no quarrel with the stockman in front of him. 'Go to your white men,' he says, 'and tell all the black men who work for them that we do not wish to harm them. We want only to free ourselves and our country. Tell all the black people you meet to come and join us. Now is the time to do battle if we are to defend what is ours and keep it.'

He turns away. There is still work to be done. The stockman, Nigger, sits his horse under the trees and wonders what to do. At last, in desperation, he makes up his mind and lunges for freedom. Leaning low over his horse's neck, at a mad gallop he breaks for open country. Sandawara grinning, sends a shot whistling after him. There's still work to be done.

IV

Fred Edgar, the boss of the group, hears the shooting and shudders. He doesn't want to be shot and, scared of niggers, has an unholy fear of being transfixed by one of their long, cruel, multi-barbed spears. It gives him the willies just thinking of it. The silence following a single last shot conjures up the memory of a stockboy transfixed by one of those wicked spears. The savage writhed for an hour, clawing at the grass clumps with bloody fingers. No, sir, he determines, he won't let that happen to him, and he turns his horse and spurs off like any retreating general.

He thunders up to the waggon and halts. What to do now? He waits indecisively until Nigger gallops up to blurt out his story. His mind thuds to a decision even before the black man has finished detailing the fight.

'Unyoke the bullocks quickly you black bastards,' he yelps and scrambles up into the waggon for more weapons.

'Here, you two, take these rifles, grab plenty of bullets. Step on it, those blood-thirsty devils will be here in no time.' The mental image of the thrusting spear tearing into his body almost causes him to retch. 'Right,' he yelps on. 'You boys stay with the waggon. Shoot anyone who comes near, savvy?'

His two workers earning a wage of sugar, flour and tobacco dubiously nod their heads, not liking it one bit.

'I'm off to Lukin's station for help,' their boss splutters, his nerve on the point of breaking. 'Get police, no worries,' he shouts in despair. And he's up and away at a flogging gallop. No bloody sir, he isn't hanging around for any black cur to slither his guts. Just the thought makes him rake the sides of his mount. Faster, faster! Edgar leans over the neck of his horse, wishing it had wings to fly him far beyond range of any spear.

The two black stockmen look after their fleeing commander.

Sambo says to his mate with a broad grin: 'He's sure going pretty fast.'

Nigger grins in return: 'He sure is.'

His mate's grin broadens. 'Well, Nigger, you're the brave one and can look after this waggon. You just stay here, I'm after old boss. Where he goes, I follow.'

'I'll stay and fight the whole lot off,' the brave one replies in dismay, shaking in his boots.

Sambo claps his hands and climbs on to the waggon. He finds a bottle of gin, breaks the neck and takes a deep swallow. 'You do that,' he says, passing the bottle down to his mate.

They quickly finish it, then stand and look towards the waterhole. 'Someone's coming,' Nigger says in a trembling voice.

'It's that Eaglehawk,' his mate declares quickly grabbing another bottle from the waggon. 'See you in Derby,' he calls, leaping on to his horse and spurring away. The sun glints off the bottle held high in one hand.

'Hey, wait for me,' shouts Nigger, leaping on to his mount and tearing off after him. He definitely is not going to be killed for any white man's property.

Sandawara on Burke's horse pulls up in best cowboy style beside the deserted waggon, gives a shout of fury and dashes off in pursuit of the far off dust clouds. The chase is long and hard, but fear and trembling is more than a match for rage. Sandawara gives up when his horse flounders and goes down. His plan has almost worked, but with the escape of the white man and the stockboys the alarm will be raised.

V

A sullen, saddle-sore, limping Sandawara finally reaches the waggon late that night. His mob has already unloaded the loot. Amongst the stores are a case of whisky, rum and gin. All through the evening the fighters and warriors have been eyeing these cases and licking their lips. But they wait until their leader trudges in, then wait some more. Exhausted he slips to the ground and immediately goes to sleep.

His mob are up early next morning and with the tribes people watch for him to awake. Sandawara comes to quickly, suddenly – with the awareness that his plans must be pushed forward. He jumps to his feet, thrusting all weakness aside. A tall black figure, now grimmer than ever, he stands glowering towards the others. They have accepted him, made him their leader, and he feels the strain. He stands there, feeling responsibility weighing him down. For them and him, the leader, the white man killer, there is only one way – towards freedom or a quick return to death. He strides to the loot with springing secure steps. Doubt can never be allowed to enter. His face, the whites describe it over and over again as primitive and bestial, is tense and grim, fierce with the pent up anger within. His plans have not succeeded. He reaches the stores. His eyes search for only one treasure – guns! This is what he needs, just as he needs willing hands able to use them. And there are guns.

He carefully examines them: three Winchesters (his favourite ·weapon), two double-barrelled shotguns (of little worth), a Schneider rifle (with which he's not familiar), a half dozen revolvers (which he disdains) and, best of all, four thousand rounds of ammunition, canisters of shot and powder, lead for bullets, bullet moulds and cartridge caps. He smiles in grim satisfaction and turns. His smile meets that of Captain, but the leader cannot loosen his newly acquired stiffness and go and slap his old comrade on the back. A leader is alone, and he stands there, his smile slowly fading in the light of admiration from his mob. Now they know how right he's been to ambush the waggon to get these guns. A leader must be constantly right or he goes down – goes down in Ellewara's frown. Sandawara already feels the tension that will call his moves, that will give him strength and dissipate his strength. Solidarity, he understands, will collapse at the first sign of weakness on his part, at the first defeat, unless, unless discipline is forged and an army formed. An army able to match the police bullet for bullet. He knows nothing of the British empire with its thousands of soldiers. He is only a man defending his and his people's space.

Sandawara distributes the arms to his mob. To the faithful Captain he hands over the heavy Schneider. The man runs his hand over the heavy metal barrel, then sits to examine his new weapon. To those who can use guns, he gives guns. There are now more weapons than men trained to handle them. Sandawara orders his more experienced men to teach others at once. There is so little time for him to form an army out of his people, naked and warm and impulsive. He watches the recruits fire their new weapons and he feels a dread of the cold white police touch his heart. Must he strive to forge an army of killers to match that of his enemies? Yes, and already he regrets the letting free of Georgy. For certain, the alarm's been raised and the police are riding towards the camp. So little time to train his men. So little time, but they must be trained.

He pushes these thoughts away and separates a good supply of tobacco and food for his band who in the months ahead must bear the full brunt of the fighting. In the long months of struggle ahead they'll need every scrap of food they can hoard and every bullet and pinch of powder. Then, in a leadership gesture, Sandawara gives the rest of the supplies to the people – the tribes who have been flocking to him as the breathless news ripples across the land.

More and more people stride in on long naked legs to join this mighty gathering of the last free people of black Australia. Proud and boastful, they sing how they have laid the white man low. The news ripples further and further out. They dispute for the stores Sandawara has given to them, butcher the cattle and eagerly watch the men on the firing range. Precious ammunition is being wasted, but it must be. Many of these men have never owned a scrap of iron before, let alone weapons forged from it. Sandawara watches and urges. Weeks of training are necessary if his men are to stand up to the police – who are already forming a huge patrol to track him down. His spies bring him news of it and he waits and makes his plans. The patrol leaves Derby and he knows how little time remains for training. He must form a plan of battle – a dream time lassitude, a fatal weakness born from a lifetime of being one with the Law flowing through him, his people and his earth, drifts him away from all struggle. What is, is; and is not to be fought with and changed. Strength flows away and he lets his impatient followers broach the alcohol.

A part of his mind knows that the poison should be fed to the earth where it can do no harm, but the surge of the dreamtime washes everything away. He lets the liquor be passed around among his people, unaccustomed to any sort of drug. He should stop it, but hell exists deep within his mind. He has known the viciousness of the white man – thus comes despair and the desire to experience to the full a moment or two of heightened life before death.

He drinks deeply of the whisky, feeling the warmth spreading like a fever through his numb body. The ways of the white men begin to prevail in the gorge. The natural disciplines, the obedience to the Law, passed down from the very dawn of humanity, disappears from the river flat.

Scenes as riotous as in old England erupt in shrieks and cries of alcohol pain kicking out in spasmodic violence. Usually, the people make small fires, a few sticks of wood burning in a scooped out hole, now huge fires like beacons are encouraged to blaze up out of control. The cliff faces dance maniacally in the flames and the shadows cast by the leaping intoxicated men and women. Cattle are speared, slaughtered and hacked in a sudden excess of food. Pieces are flung onto the flames to be seared, then scooped out and eaten half raw. Shrieking men and women gorge themselves to the full and fling the remains to the snarling dogs. Bedlam comes to cackle beside the pool. The water quivers. Sandawara sits alone and silent, lost within himself. This is his earth, his people and the white man's hell.

A frenzied capering begins. Sticks click out a disjointed rhythm, feet lurch out steps gone awry. Sandawara broods on death. Yells and shouts. Insults are flung and the tribes separate. Warriors are warriors and, lost in excess, have no law. Sandawara wanders to the poolside to brood while beyond him a battle rages. A rifle shot is lost in the boom of a shotgun. Ellewara likes sounds like thunder, blasts like lightning bolts. He believes a shotgun is more powerful than a rifle. Drunken courage, a louder boom then the deadly crack of a rifled barrel. Fighters fight and spears are hurled. Screams and curses while Sandawara dreams of disciplined warriors returning the white man volley for volley. He comes to to find his people raging, enacting the first orgy of defeat. They must be stopped, but he drifts away.

Then from out of the darkness, from the direction of the pool a strange but familiar humming begins to murmur. It rises and rises until it is a roar drowning out the screams of drunkenness. One by one, then in twos and threes the men stop and wonder. They know the sound. Suddenly a single flash of lightning splits the sky, instantly followed by a clap of thunder. An old man mutters fearfully, 'Ingaruko'. The word passes among the initiated men. The women and children cower at the fires as a storm rushes down to pelt them out with rain. 'Ingaruko – the rainbow snake – is unhappy at us,' the whisper passes beneath the continuing steady roar coming from the direction of the pool.

It calls to the men and slowly in dread they make their way towards the poolside. Behind them a low keening comes from the women. The rain, lashed by a twisting wind, sweeps through the gorge. Ingaruko is angry because his laws have been broken.

The men collect at the water's edge and nearby they see a soft rainbow light pulsating without strength from a dark figure. It is Sandawara. The men creep towards their leader and the strange roar dies away leaving only the sound of the rain and wind and thunder. Beyond them, the fires sizzle out. A lightning flash strikes a tree right next to where Sandawara is sitting and fire runs down the trunk. In amazement and fear they seem to see a huge serpent wrapped about the bod y of their leader. It writhes about his body. 'A place of strong magic and a mapan of strong magic,' the men whisper and back away to the main camp. There they get the women and children and move away to the shelter of the cliff face. No one talks of what he has seen. Such things should not be spoken about except by those able to understand them through a long and constant discipline.

The rain hisses down and fades away at the dawn leaving the people wet and cold. But it has washed away the stains of the recent conflict. Sandawara awakes at the poolside. He remembers nothing of the night. His mind instantly falls on to planning his next move in defence of his earth.

SIX

LOVE AND GUNS

In the large room at the crashpad Greg stands talking to Jane. A fat candle, a molten artistic blob melting down into a bowl, flickers in the middle of the floor. It throws some light and moves shadows on the walls. Sally sits on the mattresses feeling bored. She fiddles with the transistor, trying to get a clear sound from it. She can't. Greg's dismantling and reassembling hasn't helped. In disgust the girl flings the radio at the wall. The sound clears for a minute and a song rushes out:

> I fought the law and the law won.
> I needed money 'cause I had none,
> I fought the law and the law won.

The sound blurs and the radio mutters on in a Nungar mumble of protest.

Muscles puts his arm around Jane and pulls her against his chest. 'Hey, none of that,' the girl protests automatically, trying to pull away.

'None of what?' the youth replies, sticking his hand under her shirt. It slithers in between them and grabs a breast. Jane pushes herself tightly against his chest and wriggles against him. His other hand slides down her jeans and latches on to her arse. 'Love you, baby,' he says breathlessly the line out of some pop song, not knowing or caring if it's true or not.

He tugs her towards the mattresses. Ignoring Sally they tumble on to them with a thump. She looks at them and pouts. How come Jane always gets the attention and has all the fun.

'Hey, none of that,' automatically protests Jane as she feels her jeans being unzipped. 'Hey,' she says softly as she feels his fingers going into her.

'Love you, baby,' the youth recites, kissing her unskilfully.

'Uhuh,' the girl answers as she relaxes and begins to caress his back. After all, she does like Greg and there's nothing else to do.

The youth manages to get the girl on to her back. He gets off her jeans with a lot of help, then plunges ahead. He bangs away and Jane lies beneath him wondering why this activity is supposed to be wonderful. Sally stares at her friend jealously. No one ever takes any notice of her. Why haven't they got a telly in this place? She doesn't want to sit there watching them do it all night. She wants it done to her too.

A despondent Gary listlessly enters the room. His eyes widen when he sees what is going on. Sally, driven to desperation, smiles at him. He forgets his many problems and goes and plonks himself down next to her. Greg and Jane's heavy breathing and thump, thump rhythm make him randy. A crashpad did have its advantages and this is one of them. He looks at the girl beside him. On the thin side but good for a round or two. Gary moves against her, hoping she is willing.

'Ain't anything to do here,' Sally complains, pressing against him. 'Why don't you have a telly?'

'Arrh, there's a lot to do around here. I'm always rehearsing,' he replies, nudging her in the side.

'Yeah, maybe you are, but what about me, I don't rehearse anything. I want a telly to watch,' she demands. 'Ain't nothing to do here?' she hints.

'We can always do what they're doing,' Gary takes the bait.

'What, that?' the girl says scornfully.

'Yeah, that,' answers Gary, tired of so much dialogue. He clasps her child breasts and gives them a squeeze.

Sally giggles. This encourages him to undo her shirt and tweak her nipples. She giggles again. At last she's getting some attention. The youth's other hand spreads flat on her belly, then dips into her pants. It begins a slow slither down the side of her pants, around her hips and around to the inside of her thigh. She gasps in delight or dismay (she's not sure which) when his hand reaches the tenderest part of her. Sally hasn't really got past the fumbling stage before. Well, once or twice and then she hadn't found it much fun. It was something to endure and part of life.

Beside them Greg steadily pumps away on Jane. She moans and pulls the youth tightly to her. He plunges and gasps, sucks in a lungful of air, makes a final thrust and falls limply on her. His limbs are twitching. 'Mmmm, that was good,' the youth whispers, remaining on top of her without withdrawing. The girl feels his weight pressing down on her. It becomes unbearable and she wriggles out from under him, pushing against the back of Sally who's having second thoughts about doing it. Resisting, she curls herself into a ball and Gary gives up the struggle to get off her pants. He tries to straighten her body.

Jane sees her resistance and calls out: 'Hey don't be a silly, silly. You'll get to like it after a while.' She reaches down Greg and begins fondling him. 'It's fun,' she declares, moving her hand up and down, feeling him swelling in her fist.

'Yeah, it's fun,' Gary declares, grabbing one of the girl's hands and pressing it against his crutch. Her hand lies there. Beneath it she feels his hardness. At least, that was funny, she thinks.

'You're too big for me. It'll hurt too much,' she protests as she feels his size, but while she is talking she's changing her position so that the youth can slide her pants off. Naked from the waist down, she changes her mind again and holds her legs tightly together.

'Come on, it's nice,' Gary whispers, massaging her thighs. Her legs open and his hand moves between them.

Next to them Greg has mounted Jane again. She moans a little as he enters her and begins pumping. Her legs cross over his back arid pull him right into her. The youth holds himself up on his elbows and finds a natural rhythm. He moves with long, slow even strokes that have her gasping like a fish pulled from the ocean.

Gary feels up Sally until she becomes wet, then he slowly moves his body until he kneels between her legs. Aroused, Sally glances down at the hard length of his prick about to enter her. Awkward in his movements, the youth puts his full weight on her and she protests until he raises himself on his elbows. She wants to tell him to get on with it. Her body suddenly begins to twitch in spasmodic tics. Gary manipulates a hand and pinches the girl's rigid and swollen nipples. She begins to moan and move under him. Instinctively her hand goes down to his cock and she pulls him down and guides him in. He begins to move and suddenly Sally decides she likes it.

Rita comes to the doorway and her eyes widen in surprise as she sees what is happening. She watches for a long minute, then turns and dashes back to the kitchen.

'Hey, they're making out in the next room, let's go in and join them in the fun,' she calls excitedly to Rob. 'Bet we can show them a thing or two.'

'No, I don't want to ruin this curry I'm cooking. Gary got me the recipe. It has to be stirred every minute or so.'

'Oh, leave that old cooking and let's get fucking. It'll be fun all together. We've never done it before in a group. Come on, don't be a spoilsport.'

'No, got to add some more spices now,' Rob says, reaching for some freshly ground black pepper.

'Nasty,' the girl grins, coming to him with a fist raised. Her hand opens and she touches his face, then his lips. Her hand moves over his chin and tickles down his neck. It creeps under his shirt and slides down his chest undoing button after button until it reaches his belt which it unbuckles. Rita unzips him, but Rob pulls away to take up a spoon and stir the stew. The girl lets her body droop against his. One of the things that really turns her on is his seeming reluctance to screw. Her fingers grasp and squeeze hard. Rob's body arches and quivers under the impact of her strong fingers. She grins, having won again. The girl is anything but gentle as her hand moves, clutching strongly and forcefully. She increases the tempo of the movement and his arm comes up to hold on to her. He hugs her to him and pants out that he loves her. Rita realises that he's about to come and stops, but does not relax her hold. She's really determined to get him right off this time.

In the other room Gary has ground past his climax and stopped. 'How was it?' he asks the girl. 'It didn't hurt a bit, did it?'

'Is that all?' the girl replies, feeling how wet she is below. 'Can't you do it anymore?'

'I can try,' he says, but finds himself limp. Sally grabs him and gets him up. She tugs him on top of her and he plunges deep within. The girl gives a cry of pleasure. 'Gee, that's so nice,' she moans, pushing her bony groin hard against him.

Gary doesn't answer. He hasn't had sex in a long while and is determined to make up for it. He rocks on to a pop song roaring in his head.

Sally quivers under the thrust of his adolescent body. Her body feels glued to his and rises and falls with his rhythm. She hopes that it'll go on and on, though she's a little scared that his cock will rip her apart.

Greg continues his slow even strokes that carry him on and on, rising and falling in mini-climaxes. It's the first time he's had more than a quickie and is amazed at himself. He stops, then begins again, not knowing that the girl is almost exhausted with pleasure. She decides she loves the youth as she lies enjoying the sudden speeding up of his rhythm. With a guttural roar like the sound of some animal, he gives a last plunge into her body and goes limp in her arms. She feels the hot stickiness and knows that it is over for awhile. Greg rolls off her and lies panting at her side.

'That was real good,' Jane tells him, looking into his eyes. That instant Greg decides he loves her.

Next to them Gary gasps and sucks in the air as if he can't get enough of it. Sally wonders what's the matter with him, then squirms herself as something starts to happen in her body. She grinds against him, moaning and whimpering as she drains him of all his strength and energy. Then she lies there quivering from head to foot as he slumps on her, then rolls off. Sally feels between her legs and makes a face. 'I'm all icky,' she whispers.

In the kitchen Rob has forgotten all about his cooking. The only thing on his mind is the hand of Rita. He wants her to do it to him for ever. 'More,' he almost shouts. But she stops and he moans and reaches down to force her hand along.

The girl resumes the movement, clutching him with an iron fist. Her movement speeds up. Rob hurts with pleasure. His body begins to quiver. Then she stops and he moans in longing. Timing his ecstasy, she stops and starts, building him up to a terrific climax. She times the end. Her fingers stroke him. His body rhythmically jerks to her strokes and at last a long arc of hot fluid shoots out. She squeezes the last drop out. He sags against her and she hugs him to her.

'You and your old curry,' she whispers, 'that'll teach you. Have a rest for in a minute or two I'll want to get it off.'

The smell of something burning fills the kitchen, but Rob doesn't care. The girl starts feeling him and he begins to get randy again.

II

Greg rolls over and drifts off into sleep, Jane yawns and curls against him. Gary suddenly begins to worry about what has happened. Sally is just a kid and you can go to jail for carnal knowledge of a minor. He moves away from the scene of the crime who is ready for another round. He brushes off her hand and wants to get up and run. He begins to worry about what is happening in the crashpad itself. The vibes are becoming heavier and heavier. He wishes that everyone would go walkabout and leave him in peace. It's his place and he's responsible for everything happening there. Something brushes his behind and he brushes it away. Sally's timid hand returns to rest on his belly. A finger begins to circle his. belly button. He twists away, wondering how much time they give you for fucking a kid. Sally becomes impatient. She wants to do it again. It didn't last long enough last time. Just look how long Greg had done it to Jane.

'Don't you want any more?' she suddenly demands, deciding she doesn't like this bloke so much, even though he's a singer in a band – that is if he is. She decides to get Jane to find out more about him from Greg.

Gary's sense of alarm and despondency disappears as he feels himself becoming aroused again. He pushes Sally's hand down. It lies on him flat and inert. Neither of them speak or move. The warmth of her hand has an effect. He moves his body and sighs as he finds her clutching his crumpled flesh.

Curiously Sally toys with his limp and slippery moistness. She feels it begin to expand in her fingers. Beside her, the youth begins to pant. Her fingers flutter, tantalising him back to life. She feels him big and hard in her fist and knows he's able to begin again.

'There, I knew you'd want some more,' the girl says, giving him a squeeze which moves her hand up and down. 'Hey, that's funny,' she exclaims in mock surprise.

'Love you,' Gary gasps, kissing her quickly on the lips.

'Gee, it's funny,' Sally smiles, experimenting by tightening and relaxing her fist. She gives an extra hard squeeze and feels him leap in her hand. He rolls on top of her and for the second time she enjoys him. He takes longer to come and midway through the girl feels her whole body begin to shake. She twists about, writhing under his remorseless thrusting, and a cry rushes from her lips. It goes on and on and she comes again just at the end. Contentedly she snuggles up to the youth already hoping that he'll recover for another bout.

'That was something,' she whispers· to him. 'I'm starting to enjoy this. It's almost as good as telly.'

Gary's desire has been replaced by his fears. He inches away, as far as he can get without lying on the filthy floor.

'I've had enough,' he declares in a rush. 'I don't want anymore. I've got to get up and have a shower. Just remembered that I've got to see this guy about the band.'

He leaps to his feet and runs out of the room before the girl can protest. She lies angrily alone, wishing for someone to hold on to. Jane always has all the luck. She lies in the flickering light of the candle and wonders why life is so good one minute and so flat the next.

Someone comes into the room and she looks across at Alan. His eyes sweep around taking the scene in.

'Everything all right?' he says, grinning to the lonely Sally, the only one awake.

Her hopes rise and she yawns as she replies: 'I suppose so. At least it was a while ago.'

'Those two are snoozing. Could use a few winks myself,' the youth declares, starting to pull off his clothes. He piles them on the floor, then adopts his Sandawara pose in front of Sally's adoring eyes. She wonders what he'll be like.

'I'll just hop in beside you,' Alan says lying down next to her. The girl has a lump in her throat that stops her from answering. Automatically her thin arms open to clasp the youth's tough, hard, brown body that is so different from Gary's. She moves her hands along his backbone and nuzzles her face against his shoulder. He turns to her and she wants to kiss him. She is a little frightened at her audacity as she does so. A tremor quivers through her body. Alan's the greatest and now he's in her arms sucking at her tongue and giving her goose bumps. Won't Jane be jealous!

Alan smiles at the girl's horniness. Having been seduced by an older woman when he was thirteen and continued on with her until fifteen, he's a more experienced lover than Gary. He bends his face to her small breasts and his lips encircle a nipple. His tongue tickles and plays with it until Sally feels that she can't bear another minute of the exquisite torture. She shrugs her breast away from his questing lips.

'You've got such cute little breasts,' Alan says with a grin, his hands moving to cup them. 'Just think, they're like peaches now, but in a few years time they'll be melons.'

She begins to make a saucy reply, but his mouth is hard against hers. She gasps as his tongue flickers through her lips. His hands begin stroking the velvet softness of her young girl's body. She responds by reaching down to the place which throbs with a special ecstasy. His mouth begins to move over her, opening and closing at each stop on the journey south. She squirms against him as his firm white teeth nip at her skin. The girl wants all of him and twists away from his arms. She rolls on to her back pulling him with her.

Alan finds that the foreplay is at an end. His hands spread the girl's thin legs. Unconsciously she arches her body to let him slip into her. Her legs circle him as she raises her body to meet him. They fall into rhythm and Sally decides that this is much better than telly. Then her body jumps and bucks. She feels the liquid warmth of him spurt deep within her before he slumps with a moan on her. She too pants, but her hips still move and Alan begins to move on her again. She feels his hardness probe her and she wants it to go right through her and out of her mouth. Suddenly the ceiling and floor seem to meet. She gives a scream and her mind goes blank for an instant. Alan stops and raises himself on his elbows and knees. She makes a great effort and sits up. They kiss in affection.

'Wow, that was too much,' Alan grins, quickly recovering from his fucking.

'Wow, that was the best one tonight,' the now not-so-innocent girl smiles. 'It was worth waiting for.'

'What have you been doing all day?' the youth asks.

'Nothing much, just sitting around waiting for something to happen. There should be a telly here, then we would have something to do when we weren't doing this.'

'Don't worry, soon things will be a lot better. I've got plans for a place where we can all live together properly.'

'That'll cost a bit of money,' the girl says.

'Yeah, I'm thinking of getting it from a bank.'

'They won't give you any,' the girl says in scorn.

'We can always rob one of them.'

The girl stares at him wide-eyed and he goes on to try and explain things to her. 'It's for the revolution,' he tells her and is met with a look of incomprehension.

'What's that mean? Don't know any big words.'

'Well, if you want to change things quickly, you have to fight. This guy told me all about it. He used to say that we're all brothers and sisters and there should be no bosses.'

'What's that got to do with us? Lots of people try to tell me things, too, and I just don't listen. This teacher he used to talk to me some and then one day he tried to take me behind the bushes. They always have some reason or other. That's the way they are and it doesn't bother me.'

'Yeah, but this is different,' Alan tries to explain. 'The main thing is that the white people took everything from us Nungars and now we want some of it back. It belongs to us and we want it back. They won't give it to us and so we'll take it.'

Alan's the greatest and so the girl listens. 'You mean if we want a telly, we should go out and knock one off?' she asks. 'That's a good idea. We can get up and go and get one now, then it won't be so boring sitting around with nothing to do.'

The youth starts playing with her nipple as he tries to get across to her some of his ideas. 'Well, I don't mean exactly that,' he replies. 'My idea is to set up a youth hostel and to set it up we need money and the only way to get money is to steal it.'

'Yeah, I know that,' the girl says, tugging at his pubic hair. 'But a hostel is just like one of those homes they put you in. I don't like them places. They lock you up and you're not supposed to talk to boys and have to obey all those rules.'

'This one'll be different. It'll be ours and we'll be running it. We'll all be together in one big happy family.'

'That might be all right. There'll be a T.V. set there, won't there?'

'We'll have everything there,' Alan grandly declares, deciding that there's been enough talk for the night. He thinks of Ken Rawlings and decides to go and listen to him more. He likes the way the man speaks and can learn from him.

The side gate slams and the door rattles open, then closes with a bang. A less derelict Charly walks into the funky room. He peers around the gloom and says: 'You better watch out, the cops'll raid this place one day and take you all in.' He finds the guitar, picks it up and begins to tune it.

'Heard this old song the other day, I like it,' he says as he begins to sing:

Yaweee, yahaaweee, my brownskinned baby they takim away.

As a young stockman, I used to ride
My quiet pony around the countryside;

In a native camp, I'll never forget,
A young black mother, her cheeks all wet.

Yaweee, yahaaweee, my brownskinned baby they takim away.

Between her sobs I heard her say:
Police been take my baby away,
From white man boss that baby I had,
Why he let them take baby away?

Yaweee, yahaaweee, my brownskinned baby they takim away.

To a children's home, a baby came,
With new clothes on and a new name;
Day and night he would always say:
Mummy, mummy why they take me away?

Yaweee, yahaaweee, my brownskinned baby they takim away.

The child grew up and had to go
From the mission home he loved so.
To find his mother he tried in vain,
Upon this earth they'll never meet again.

Yaweee, yahaaweee, my brownskinned baby they takim away.

The four kids sit up with misty eyes. They remember their mothers and how they have either been taken away from them or run away from them. Alan can just picture his mother living on a reserve down Narrogin way. They took him and put him in a home and five times he tried to get away from it. Four times, the image of his mother drew him on, the fifth time the city beckoned and he stayed there. No one bothers him, though he supposes they can put him back inside whenever they want to.

The two little girls hug each other. They miss their families, even though they don't have a television set. The tough guy, Greg, refuses to become emotional. His father was a drunk and his mother slept with anyone. The pain of his home has long since been suppressed. He listens to the song and wonders if he and Charly can form a band. Charly is getting better since he's off the grog. The singer puts down the guitar and, without a word, leaves. Alan pulls on his clothes and goes to the kitchen to get some food. The others get up, and are pulling on their clothes when there is a loud crash at the gate.

Blam, the side door is kicked off its hinges and fourteen huge cops led by Collins and Kelly charge into the room.

'Right you kids, get against the wall. Move,' Kelly yells in his best T.V. manner. This is what it's like being a cop.

They stand against the wall and are searched. Nothing is found.

'Take them to the waggon,' Collins shouts.

The kids are hustled out and the police proceed to tear up the place in their search for any sort of contraband.

'What a pigsty. Stinks like hell,' Kelly growls to Collins.

'Those boongs like it like that,' Collins replies to Kelly.

They kick the mattresses over and create much more of a mess. Their search is fruitless. Nothing illegal at all. Collins gives a last kick at a mattress. His foot goes right through and he has to tug his leg out. Tired of the search, they glance into the empty bathroom and kitchen.

'Tidy bit of work,' Kelly says to Collins. 'Pity we can't get anything on them.'

'Yeah, but those girls are runaways. Don't know about the boy though.'

'We'll check him out at the station. At least, the raid wasn't worthless.'

III

The crashpad remains the mess the police have reduced it to in the late afternoon light of the next day, or the same day. As most of life is lived at night in the pad, it is difficult to keep track of the time and the day. The faint stutter of the dying radio inches about the room like some noisy insect. A movement at the doorway and in slinks Ron. He stands spooning corn beef from a can and gloats over the scene of chaos. His heh, heh, heh, heh cackle sounds out flat and triumphant. Finishing off the meat, he tosses the can and spoon on to the floor and slinks about the room turning over things with his toe. He finds nothing of value.

Rob enters the room and gapes at the mess. -Those pigs really root up a place, don't they,' he exclaims to Ron who nods and flashes his mirror sunglasses in his direction. 'Luckily I burnt the curry I was cooking last night. I was just cleaning out the pot when crash, bang, thud. I tell you I leapt right after Alan out of the window and hared off down the street. Rita came out after me. We sat around a coffee bar for the rest of the night, then went and had a sleep in King's Park. Do you know what happened to the others?'

Ron flashes his sunglasses negatively just as Alan prances into the place. He jerks his face around, then scratches his head. 'They've got Jane and Sally, Greg too. The girls'll be in the holding centre. We'll just have to get them out. Hope they let Greg go. He's clean and they can't book him.' He spins around, straightens the picture of Sandawara, then races off to locate the girls and the youth. He just misses Greg and Gary. Two very bedraggled youths enter. Gary who caught the tail end of the action and has hidden under a hedge for the rest of the night and the day, stares in dismay at the wreck of his place.

Greg feels a solidarity and says to him: 'Don't worry, we'll get our own back for this, just see if we don't. No one can keep a Nungar down. This isn't a setback. Just wait, soon we'll make them pay.'

The last thing Gary wants is more trouble and uneasily replies, 'Yeah, man' into the violent aura of musclehead. This is the last straw as far as he's concerned. He wants out before something worse happens. He thinks of the airforce and wonders how he'll look in uniform.

Greg stares at Ron, right into and through his sunglasses. He takes his anger out on the man. 'Hey, you, I want that forty cents you owe me,' he yells, bunching his fist and advancing on the man.

Ron hurriedly fumbles through his pockets and finds two coins. 'Just came to give it to you,' he mumbles. He's frightened of Greg because he can't spook him.

The youth takes the coins. 'Thanks, at last you've paid someone back. You're lucky I didn't take it out of your hide. I better go and check the car. Maybe the pigs towed it away or something like that. We need those wheels now. Things are coming to a head,' he declares mysteriously and menacingly.

Gary looks after him and almost shudders. He hasn't the nerve to demand the return of his car keys. That Greg could kill him! His brow wrinkles as he worries over whether Sally is detailing the events of last night to the police. They must be under age. He feels the bars closing around him. Things are not going from bad to worse, but from worse to worse, and he's trapped right in the middle of the mess.

'What're you doing here,' he turns to take it out on Ron. 'You don't belong here, you aren't welcome here. I pay the rent. This is my place and I don't want you coming here!'

'Those little girls that were here,' begins Ron. He gives a leer which makes Gary's heart sink into his boots. 'They were under age, weren't they? That's carnal knowledge, that is! They put me into the booby hatch for that. But I didn't do it. No, I was innocent. A lying little slut, just like one of them, dobbed me in. What'll happen to you when they find out? Police don't like you wogs fucking under age Aussie chicks, even Abo ones. They know what your sort are like. It'll be six months for sure. Don't worry, mate, I'll take over your pad for you and look after it real good. Maybe you'll get a year, never can tell, depends on the judge and what he thinks of your sort.'

'Ron, you know I didn't have anything to do with those girls. Alan brought them here,' the dismayed Gary replies half-heartedly. God, what'll happen to him!

'Maybe, maybe not. Just let one of them say you did and they'll believe her, not you. I know what they're like. I spent seventeen years in the loony bin for that sort of thing. At least I got a pension out of it; you'll only get a cell and a record.'

'Arrh, come on,' Rob butts in, 'nothing will happen. Those kids are all right and don't carry tales to the coppers. He's just trying to put the wind up you, Gary, just forget about it.' He tries to reassure the Anglo-Indian, but the youth feels he's in for it. Giving up, Rob goes into the kitchen to help Rita with the tidying up.

Gary tries to push his fears away. 'Yeah, Rob's right, there's nothing to worry about. Ron, you get out of my place. Nothing happened and even if it did, they wouldn't tell.'

'Wouldn't they?' Ron sneers. 'Just you wait and see.'

'Get out of here,' the youth shouts in exasperation.

'See you in jail,' the nut laughs, baring his teeth, vanishing and leaving a very unhappy Gary behind. The weight of his troubles visibly stoops his back.

An authoritative knock raps once, twice and thrice on the broken outer door. Gary starts. He knows that knock, and is in two minds about answering it. Heavy steps march along the passageway towards the room. Fatalistically, Gary waits to answer the guilt of his birth. A ramrod figure in a neat grey business suit which somehow manages to look like a uniform on the stiff body, marches to the centre of the room and stops at attention. A tightly rolled umbrella is clutched tightly to its side like an officer's wand. The man stands at ease, then begins poking at the rubbish scattered over the floor. The neat, short-haired head inclines and a closely shaven face inspects everything with a close regard to detail. The face is finally allowed to register distaste.

'Well son!' the major, ex-Indian army, raps out. 'How long are you going to torment your sister and myself like this? Each night we pray to God that you'll come to see the error of your ways and regain your senses. You're a disgrace to the whole family and the Anglo-Indian community. For one moment place yourself in my shoes and imagine how I feel when someone meets me and asks about you. What am I to say, my God, what am I to say – that my only son, my first born, is a hippy scrounging off others and living a nasty, unclean life?'

'But, Dad,' Gary begins. A curt gesture cuts him short.

'I don't mind your sowing a few wild oats. Did the same in my youth, but this isn't the same thing. Living in a pigsty is not my idea of having a good time. Please, please, son, try to remember that we belong to a very respectable family that for generations has produced some of the best officers in the imperial services. All the male members have distinguished themselves in the service of Queen and Empire. I, myself, received the D.S.M. for bravery beyond the call of duty. I exceeded my duty, I didn't shirk it. Never in my wildest moments did I and your mother, bless her, imagine that we would have such a son. Life, my lad, is not a spot of leave from the trenches, it's a campaign and no medals are ever handed out for slackness. Just as I faced the Japs in Burma, so must you face the enemy called life and win through. The airforce is the wave of the future and now is the time to become part of that wave. I always wanted to become a flying officer myself, but never had the chance. Now I have through my one and only son. If you're lucky a war'll break out and you'll have the opportunity to distinguish yourself and earn your own command. Son, I beg you to come to your senses and be a man!'

'But Dad,' Gary tries to break in. A gesture silences him.

'You should at least stand up straight when you talk to me. A father is like a C.O. Yours is not to reason why, yours is but to do or die – that's the spirit, son! Son, airforce life will make you or break you. I know that it won't break you. You are a product of a military family going back to the Mutiny. We never let the side down and always stand ready to do our duty.'

'Yes Dad,' a subdued Gary answers. 'I see your point.'

'Excellent, at last you are coming to your senses. About time, too, I might add. Let's evacuate this pigsty and march out to fight the enemy, life, in a disciplined formation.'

'Yes Dad,' the subdued Gary answers weakly, thinking that this is as good a way out of the mess as any other. Besides, if he doesn't like the airforce, he can always desert. Consoled by this, he surrenders. 'I'm ready Dad,' he says.

'Your sister will greet your decision with tears of joy,' the major declares. 'And I, as an officer and a gentleman, extend my hand to you. As the good book says: "There is more rejoicing over the finding of one lost sheep than of ninety-nine that have not gone astray."'

The major takes off his righthand glove and extends his hand to his son. Gary takes it and endures a manly handshake. He pushes away the heretical thought that jail after all might be more endurable.

'Let's advance from this place and never retreat to it,' the soldier commands and does an about turn. He marches to the door and his son falls into step behind him. Reaching the street, they march side by side in close formation past a half-drunken Tom stumbling along and trying to remember the events of the past few days. They march past Sue who walks along firmly with an outward show of confidence, a symbol of the Aboriginal movement on the march towards equality and dignity.

Tom enters the room without noticing the shambles. He straightens a mattress and falls on it, moaning. He curls up into a ball and tries to shut out the light. Sue comes in and gasps at the mess. She calls out, 'Tom,' and the man uncurls and blinks up at her. 'What?' he manages to say.

'What on earth happened here? Looks like a cyclone's ripped through it.'

'Don't ask me, I didn't do it,' Tom groans, sinking back.

Rob enters to enlighten them. Tom doesn't care, but Sue is indignant and wants to take the matter up with the Aboriginal Legal Service. She sets to work to straighten everything up. Tom falls asleep as she works on. The place is tidier than it has ever been when Alan returns.

'Seen Greg?' he asks her.

'Think he's working on the car,' the girl replies. 'He said something about getting it ready to go and rescue Jane and Sally. It's a shame what's happened to them. They're such kids and we can take care of them. Give them a sense of direction and pride and see to it that nothing bad happens to them.'

'Seems like Greg's starting to think on his own,' Alan says, adopting his Sandawara stance. 'That's real good. We'll get the kids out and take care of them. They're our own. This is one of the reasons why we need the hostel. Too many Nungar kids are running around on the streets and getting into all sorts of trouble. They need a place to live; a place they can call home, and feel that they belong to a group. It'd change them for the better in no time. Nungars must look after Nungars,' he declares in his best Ken Rawlings manner. He's just come from visiting him. 'We don't want white people telling us what to do. We want to learn what to do and how to do it. We must change because we want to change, not have it forced on us by outsiders.'

'Yeah, yeah,' Tom mutters sarcastically from the mattress. 'Why I can't even take care of myself, let alone anyone else. Those two kids are better off inside. It'll keep them off the streets and might even stop them from becoming whores.'

Sue darts an angry glance at him and Alan ignores his words. Tom is one of those needing help and, when the hostel is a fact, he'll be helped.

'The thing to do,' Alan declares, 'is to get those kids out of that place. I've been in there and it's dead easy to climb over the side fence and into the yard. The girls'll be in a dormitory. They'll be expecting us to come and get them out. We'll strike at midnight. I know one of the kids in there and where he sleeps. He'll be able to tell us where they are. It's a cinch. Let's get the car out and get cracking. You coming, Tom?'

'Feel like a sleep,' the man replies.

'Arrh, don't cop out,' the girl sneers at him. Tom gets up and the three go out to the car.

IV

The two teenyboppers have had an enjoyable day in the home. They tell the other kids about their adventures and enjoy the impact and the envy. To the other girls they whisper about their boyfriends. The girls turn green with envy. The evening is spent in front of the telly and they really enjoy it. In bed that night they grow restless. They want to get out into the groovy adventures. They whisper about Ron and shiver delightedly. They dote on Alan. He won't leave them inside for long. By ten they're fast asleep. Just after midnight Alan's thin brown hand touches Jane's face and she instantly comes awake. She knew Alan would come. Daringly, the youth slides into her bed and hugs her to him. Quickly they make love and Jane goes all tingly.

'Wake up Sally in the same way,' she giggles to the youth. He slides off her and into the next bed.

Sally comes to as Alan enters her. Her hips begin to move with his rhythm and her bony knees clasp him to her. Quickly Alan comes and rolls off her. The dormitory is inspected by a matron every hour and it is just about time for her to make her rounds. The girls quickly pull on their clothes and creep out with their deliverer. The yard is dark and shadowy. Breathing rapidly and with their hearts in their mouths, the two teenyboppers scramble after Alan over the fence and into freedom. They leap down into the street and race to the waiting car. Jane gets in beside Greg, the driver, and punches him lightly on the arm. Greg grins and hugs her. He's happy to have a woman as his own. Sally squeezes into the back seat beside the sour smelling Tom. She had hoped that Gary would've been along and is dismayed to have this strange man beside her. He doesn't say a word to her. She looks across to Sue as Alan gets into the front and sits beside Jane. She's happy to have boys on either side.

'Hi, Sue,' Jane says, smiling back over her shoulder. 'Glad you got us out of that old place. We were getting sick of it. Of course we get to watch telly, but there's better things to do, isn't there?'

'Yeah, that's right,' Sue replies. 'There's a lot of things better than sitting in front of that idiot box. Alan will tell you all about them. One day we'll have our own place and you'll be there with all of us.'

'Will it have a telly?' Jane cuts in.

'Of course it will, silly,' Sally retorts. 'It'll have everything, just like a real home. Alan told me so last night.'

'What's a real home?' Jane asks wistfully.

'Like you see on telly,' her now more aggressive friend answers, as the motor starts and Greg surges off in a show intended for Jane.

'What will we do now?' Sue asks Alan.

'Let's go home and get some sleep,' Tom jerks out.

Alan answers Sue. 'If we're to get the money to set up our own place soon, we'll have to hit a bank. Guns are needed if we are to make that cash withdrawal,' he grins.

Tom sinks back with an inaudible groan. He's forgotten all about the job. He feels the need for a drink, but this late at night and with these people, he has no chance of scoring one.

'You know that gun shop in East Perth?' Alan goes on. 'I was in there the other day and noticed it hasn't got an alarm system. Of course they take all the guns out of the window at night and lock them behind a grille, but Greg picked up some bolt cutters today and I bet we can get through that in no time. Let's go there. You know the way, Greg.'

'Spot on,' Greg agrees, glancing across at Alan. He drives along carefully, obeying all the traffic laws and some of his own invention. In front of him a shiny set of drums begin to quiver. He imagines himself seated before them laying down a solid beat. The two teenyboppers look large-eyed at each other. Just out and the adventures are beginning. When they get back into that home won't they have a lot to tell the girls. The best thing will be about making love right in the dormitory. They can see the awe filled faces of the other kids as they lay it on thick.

The car moves sedately along the street. The night is bright, but not too light. A quarter moon floats, a smile among the stars. The kids feel the special tingle of adventure urging them on. Tom, a man, feels that he's about to lose something he's never had. Sue sits away from him as does Sally. Alone in the middle of the seat, he faces the loneliness of a prison cell. If only he could get some enthusiasm going, if only he didn't feel so down. A thought flashes: he'll give up the grog – but what'd he do without it? Join Alan in his madcap schemes. Well, he's doing that already, isn't he? Oh God, he needs a drink. Then a further thought comes up: why not join A.A. and escape from all this? The thought scares him. He'd need a drink to get the courage to attend a meeting. He gives up, the only place he can be is in this car and he'll have to ride on.

The vehicle slowly wheels past the gun store and pulls up in the shadow of a building.

The hyperactive Greg immediately leaps out and gets the bolt cutters from the boot. Tom waits in the car, but the others scramble out and walk down a lane that turns behind the shop. Silence, broken only by the distant hum of a few cars. The moon lightens the open spaces and deepens the shadows. It's thrilling!

The back door is securely fastened with an antique padlock. Muscles manipulates the cutters and with a snip and the clatter of metal striking concrete, the way is unbarred. Alan tries the door while the two teenyboppers stare in fascination. 'Terrific,' Sally whispers to Jane as the door swings open and they move into the back room. Sue carefully shuts the door behind them. They can't see a thing and no one's brought along a torch. Alan feels the wall and touches a switch. The sudden light tears away the darkness and leaves them blinking. Luckily, the door leading into the shop is closed. None of the light seeps through to betray them.

Alan grins in happiness as he looks about and sees cabinets filled with firearms. Now they won't have to go into the shop. He goes to the cases and finds them unlocked. He and Greg pull out high- powered rifles and stack them beside the door. Six 22s, a 30/30 and a 303. Lastly, he finds a pistol in a table drawer together with a few boxes of ammunition. Remembering Sandawara and his need for bullets and more bullets, he looks around for ammo for the rifles. There's a whole case of 22 cartridges, but none for the heavy rifles. Disappointedly he adds four more light bore guns and throws aside the heavy guns, one of which is a Winchester just like Sandawara's. Now to get them to the car.

Greg goes to the door and Alan turns off the light. The door opens and closes. They wait and hear the sound of a vehicle starting up and coming along the lane. It stops at the door and Alan grins.

They go through the door and open the boot. Silently and quickly they load the guns and ammo, then get into the vehicle. Greg deftly reverses it back down the lane and into the street. They move off. Alan is elated. At last, they are getting ready for action. Tom sits silently in the front seat beside Greg.

'Where we off to now?' the driver calls back to Alan sitting between Sally and Sue. Both girls sit right next to him.

'Let's go to the bush and get in some practice,' Alan replies. 'No use having guns and not knowing how to use them. There's a place about fifty miles along the York road. No one around for miles and we can shoot as much as we want to.'

'I know the road,' Greg says, smiling. He been out hunting many a time and can impress Jane with his shooting skill.

'Alan,' Sue says, 'I've been out shooting and can teach the kids.'

'That's good. Greg and I can get in a little practice. What about you, Tom?'

'I've been up north after dingo scalps,' Tom replies, getting over his dourness, or at least some of it. He likes shooting. 'I'm a pretty good shot. I just hope that place you know is right in the bush. The sound of a rifle travels for miles.'

'Arrh, come on Tom,' Sue retorts. 'Alan'll know a good place. He's not going to get us into trouble, are you, Alan?'

'Not me, I don't want to muck up my plans. This place is about twenty miles along a dirt road leading to nowhere. The only thing that can go wrong is the car.'

'And that won't,' a confident Greg asserts, switching on the radio and finding a country and western station. He wonders whether he should mention the band idea to Charly, or not.

The car rushes through the sweet West Australian night, the scent of eucalypts blowing through the open windows. Even Tom brightens up as the lights of the city are left far behind. The clean country air knocks the last of the alcohol fumes out of his head. A piss stop and he takes the opportunity to get one of the rifles out of the boot. They move on and he deftly strips the gun. It's a Remington and he values the feel of a quality weapon.

SEVEN

WOMEN AND TRAITORS

Noorak broods over his fire, watching the flickering flames eat away at the sticks. Fire is the all consuming passion of Sandawara to free his land. Alan glides into the firelight. The youth is not alone. Sue is beside him. She looks down at the old black man, so fragile, so ancient, so lost in his dreams that he isn't aware of their presence. Alan places before him the customary offerings of a bottle of sweet wine and soft hamburger meat. Silently, they stand before the bossman, then sit across the fire from him. Sue feels shivery and a little frightened. She glances at Alan. His eyes are on the old man. She detects some of the feeling the youth has for the elder and wonders. Alan continually surprises her. Just a kid, but something more. He strides into the future dragging his group with him. His intensity of purpose frightens her more than a little. Where will it all end? Will they ever get their hostel? Everything is hazy except that she knows Alan will go places as he gets older; but will his followers, will she, go there with him? She looks from the youth to the old man. What could possibly connect these two? – the dashing city youth and an old, old man lost in dreamtime visions of a lost culture. She remembers stories that her mother told about these old black men, how they can sing people – either to death or, if a woman, to get her to come to them. Has this old man the power? Has he sung Alan to him for some obscure reason? She'll never know the answer. Women are excluded from such knowledge.

'This your woman, son?' the old man says, startling them with his sudden whisper. His voice is as the rustling of leaves, the sigh of the wind over the earth – a felt thing like the hush of the earth before the emergence of the new day's sun. 'This your woman, son?' he asks again, his hand seeking out for the hamburger meat.

'Yes, Granddad,' Alan replies after making a quick decision.

The old man chews, then begins to speak: 'Kangawara was the woman of Sandawara.'

The two young people settle into the quiet of the night to listen to the voice recreating the old legends ...

Once Sandawara descended alone into the cave of the Wandjina, the place of his ancestral spirits. From the walls, the ghostlike shapes gaze down upon him. He had been wounded, not once, but four times and he needed to recover. Deep within his earth, he rested, letting the strength of his living ancestors flow into him and heal his wounds. The police surprised and shot him and he has been saved from them by his woman, Kangawara. With the strength of desperation she tugged his heavy body to the entrance of the cave and while everyone else thought him dead, she tended his wounds, holding his stricken body in her arms and crooning over him. She let his tribe think him dead. On her forays for food, if anyone questioned her, she hung her head and did not answer. A dead person's name cannot be spoken for a set period and they took her silence as a fact of his death. Even the white men believed it. They know the custom.

Black women are faithful to their men, not in body but in spirit. Ellewara's woman, Wandara, saved him from certain death. One time as she finished cooking her man's meal and brought it to him and waited, as is the custom, to be given her share, Kangawara and a group of women went to stand guard while their men rested after a raid. Getting her food, Wandara began to eat when there was a long, piercing cry of warning from Kangawara. Again it rings out and the men leap for their weapons. The sound of racing hooves pounds towards the camp. The freedom fighters, avoiding battle, race away. Behind them the coarse yells of the white men shriek and the crack crack of revolvers fling Ellewara to the ground. He claws for his weapon in rage. His woman leaps to help him to his feet, unafraid of the bullets whistling around her. She tugs him to a patch of scrub and they take cover as the enemy swirl up. The couple flatten down into a narrow grass-lined gutter as horses dash past. Ellewara wants to get up and make off to the hills. He believes that if he stays where he is he'll be captured. But Wandara hugs him and keeps him to the ground. She knows that her wounded man cannot outrun the police party or fight them off by himself.

'No, we stay here,' she insists. 'How can you run with that wound. Even if you do escape, they'll follow your blood trail and run you down. We'll lie low here. Let them chase the others and follow them into the hills. No one will think that a man as brave as Ellewara will hide near his enemies and refuse to fight.'

Her words have the opposite effect on him. He, Ellewara, will never hide like a dingo and refuse to give battle to the curs that surround him. His hand feels for his weapon as his woman's voice continues to urge him to remain quiet. At last with a scowl he agrees with her. It is sound advice, especially with the few bullets he has remaining. For days Wandara keeps him hidden in the gully. Always she urges him not to move. Just one track would give him away to the trackers questing about for the scent. She does the foraging for food. She looks after him and they stay hidden near the camp while all around the police hunt for him. It is only when his strength is part way restored that they sneak away into the hills.

In the same action which lays Ellewara low, Captain's woman, Terawara is captured. In the hands of the enemy she refuses to admit defeat. She can serve the cause even in captivity. A traitor black from Queensland, and thus alone in a strange country, tries to gain her confidence. After a time she lets him think that she is coming around to his way of thinking. The traitor questions her about the fight. Most of all he wants to verify that Sandawara is dead. The invaders are beginning to be hurt and they want the leader of the freedom fighters dead as much as he wants them out of his country. Terawara smiles at the man and after much hesitation finally tells him that Sandawara was shot dead in the first day's shooting. He urges her for details and she supplies them. Sandawara, badly wounded, dragged himself away from the scene of the conflict. Eventually, when his men regroup, he does not appear. They go off in search of their leader and finally find him by the smell of his decomposing body. Lamenting they take up his body and bury it. She says she did not see it herself, but has heard about it from many people. The traitor conveys the news to the white men and they smile in relief. The long insurrection is almost over. They have finally killed the chief troublemaker and all that remains is to round up his downhearted followers. Terawara smiles to herself. Sandawara is alive and even though wounded is planning more raids to keep the enemy under steady pressure.

The old man sinks into those days that are, to him, more alive than the present. His hand lifts the bottle of sweet wine to his lips. His old body warms and he murmurs on. The women recede into the background as he recounts the events surrounding their strength and their deep comradeship with the men.

Sue listens, striving to catch each and every soft word. This is the first time that she's realised that her people have a history and that they have fought and died in defence of their homeland. A bond between the past, present and future is being tied. She begins to realise that Alan seeks to become part of a tradition of resistance which began from the moment the white men invaded their land and took what was not theirs to take.

II

The invader, Alf Barnett is very conscious of the threat Sandawara poses to his holdings. A fear has swept over all the Kimberleys and no white man feels safe. Isolated settlers debate moving into the safety of fortress Derby which itself is in the grip of near panic. Rumours abound that a huge horde of hostile natives lead by the devil, Sandawara, are marching to attack the town. Frantically, special constables are created and every white man able to hold a gun is deputised to shoot legally any black they consider a freedom fighter. Heavily armed patrols of twenty and thirty men scour the land seeking the elusive Sandawara and his growing band of guerrillas. No local blacks are trusted and special trackers from Queensland are imported. Far away on the north-eastern coast, they are dragooned into service and shipped thousands of miles away from their homes. The black people of the Kimberleys treat them as outcasts and render them useless as intelligence agents. Alf Barnett decides that the imported 'boys' are useless. Though fine trackers, they'll never run the local black killers to earth. He thinks up a little scheme of his own to end the menace to his stolen property. He bribes six of his most trusted 'boys' to infiltrate the guerrilla forces. They are to discard their white fellow clothing, revert to their natural nakedness and pretend to be freedom fighters. At the first opportunity they are to assassinate Sandawara or, failing this, are to create as much havoc as possible and destroy as many firearms as they can.

The six men reluctantly leave the white fellows' camp and cautiously make their way towards liberated country. They travel towards the ramparts of the Barrier range. Away from their boss, Barnett, they begin to feel more and more isolated and in danger. As the distance between the camp and themselves widens so does the gap between them and their masters. They have learnt to say 'yes' to anything that the white man might demand, never have they been able to refuse. Now they have said 'yes' again and are on their own. Striding across the land they recount stories about the exploits of Sandawara, Ellewara, Captain and the other freedom fighters. As they near the mountain range their trepidation increases. They begin to believe that the white man, Barnett, is sending them to their deaths in punishment for some slight wrong they have committed unconsciously.

From a small group of women and children they learn that Sandawara and his band are camped in Wandjina gorge. They make their way towards it, rehearsing the story which Barnett has given to them. They are to declare that they have killed their white boss. Now as they discuss it, it seems more and more a weak fiction which can be seen through by such men as Sandawara and Ellewara. Not knowing what to do, they reach the gorge and try to assume the confident stride of true liberation fighters. They stride on, but inside they are quaking and beginning to be ashamed of their treachery. They do not like doing the dirty work for the white man safely barricaded in his camp.

The women comrades, on lookout duty, spy the six men and challenge them in shrill tones as they pass beneath. They shout their story up to the lookouts and it is accepted as is the assertion that they are volunteers coming to join the liberation movement. As they move closer to the camp they begin to pass groups of men. No one challenges them or demands an explanation. They must go to the leader and explain themselves. It is an old custom.

Sandawara's main body of men is camped down by the large waterhole which is rich in fish and waterfowl and can support a large body of people. A wild and beautiful spot, surrounded by high rugged cliffs and trees growing right to the water's edge, it has been created long ago by the Wandjina ancestors. Sandawara sits close to the bank of the pool with his Winchester across his knees. Two bandoliers criss-cross his naked chest and a cartridge belt is buckled around his narrow waist. He knows the value of ammunition, knows that a gun is useless without bullets just as a man is useless without a gun. The southern man, Captain, sits talking to him. Accepted in this land, he regards it as his new home, he squats confidently beside the leader with his Schneider close to hand. Nearby lounges Ellewara cleaning his double-barrelled shotgun. He also has a cartridge belt around his waist. It is half empty for he is running out of ammunition for his favourite weapon. All the men are naked except for the needed white man's weapons.

Nakedness is their uniform for they have discarded in contempt white fellow's clothing and gone back to their natural state.

Striving to put on a show that will convince, the six strut up to the feared men. Sandawara looks up and gazes at them. They inwardly quake and curse the white man who has sent them out into trouble and perhaps death. The leader's eyes move from one to the other. His eyes eat into their eyes. No one speaks. They feel that Sandawara knows that they are spies, assassins and saboteurs. Silence, broken only by the gentle calls of birds, the humming of insects and, from the far side of the pool, the laughter of black children as they attempt to spear a fish. The traitors look across at the kids and feel shame for what they have been forced to become. But they haven't the heart to confess and become comrades under this man who sits reading their faces as the white men read their bits of paper.

At long last Sandawara moves. He shifts his rifle. They stare into the dark muzzle pointing in their direction.

'What do you want?' the leader says coldly.

They stammer out that they wish to join his band of freedom fighters. In an endeavour to gain acceptance they describe how they have killed their boss, Barnett, and burnt his hut to the ground.

'Where are his guns?' Sandawara demands sternly. 'Men without guns are not men. You would not have left them behind.'

They look at one another and try to find an answer.

Sandawara gets them to repeat their story. He wishes to believe them for he needs every man he can get. There must be a federation of tribes if the crusade is to succeed and these men are from a different people. He listens and wants to believe, for all the tribes must forget their bickerings and march together. Then no white man will be able to remain alive in the Kimberleys. But he looks at the men and knows they lie. He says nothing.

Ellewara has seen through their lies also, but, unlike Sandawara, he does not wait for the men to admit it. He cocks his double-barrelled gun and raises it to his shoulder. The clicks of both hammers sound like thunder in the ears of the traitors.

'Do you take us for fools?' he shouts out. 'Are we blind and deaf that we do not know what the white man does? He cannot piss without us counting the number of evil-smelling drops.' Contemptuously, he looks them over. 'Dingoes are dingoes and are not to be trusted when they bark about brave deeds. I am not like Wira, the moonman, who allowed himself to be tricked by his own sons and ended up trapped in the sky. If I went out hunting and came back to tell how I killed a giant kangaroo, who would believe me? No one, unless I carried its carcase right into camp so that everyone could see it. You declare that you killed this white fellow, Barnett, and did not even think to carry off his guns and ammunition. Everyone knows the value of a gun, just as I know that the value, of lies is a quick death.'

Ellewara scowls and the six men wait for the thunder of his powerful weapon. They know that if it were loaded with wire cartridges, heavy shot or slugs bound together in lead foil and held in one compact mass by a covering of thin wire, a double blast would cut a man in two.

'Wait,' Sandawara says, getting to his feet and getting between the muzzles of Ellewara's weapon and the six men. 'We know you lie, but even though you do, we know that you belong with us and not with the white men who have sent you out to spy on us. Ellewara is too quick to kill. I want fighters, but proven ones. We must free our land and drive the white man away for ever. You have come to us with lies – now go back and make them the truth. Go quickly and kill the white man, Barnett, and bring his guns back to us. Do this or Ellewara will hunt you down and rid this land of six dingoes without the kidneys needed to be warriors and freemen. Now go and return as men.'

Without a word the traitors turn and retrace their steps. They slink along conscious of the men behind them and the guns aimed at their backs.

'You think they'll kill that white fellow now?' Ellewara shouts at Sandawara.

'Yes,' the leader replies. 'They will do it or the story of their shame will sing them to their death.'

In two days the six men return to the police camp. Barnett scowls as he hears their story that Sandawara and his band cannot be located. He curses them as misbegotten sons of the devil and decides never to trust a native again. Late the same night Barnett is a dead man and Sandawara has gained six men and three guns with ammunition.

III

The enraged police patrol, horrified at the terrorists striking in the security of their camp and escaping with guns, saddle up their horses and gallop after the tracks of the men. In their haste to return to the guerrilla camp, the six men do not cover their tracks well and the Queensland trackers can easily follow them towards the wild Wandjina gorge. A half day's journey to the gorge, the large patrol stops and sends out scouts, black men, to find out if the freedom fighters are camped there. The Queensland 'boys' gallop out and the patrol waits their return. They question anyone who knows the country and are determined to wipe the outlaw blacks out once and for all.

The Lennard river has churned this gorge right through the Napier range. In the wet season the Wandjina spirits send floods to pour in torrents between the cliff faces. In the dry season the water retreats into the sky and the deep Wandjina pool lies peacefully between the steep limestone breasts of the mountain range. This is a part of Sandawara's earth and he feels at one with it. Now it is in danger of being invaded. Enemy scouts spy out the land and note the camp. They slither back to their horses, mount and gallop with the news to the police patrol. The invaders debate how to breach the fortress and decide on a plan.

The large police party divides into four. One part rides out in a wide circle which will bring them to the northern edge of the gorge. Another part advances to take up positions along the southern edge. The two other parties are to advance from the east and west down and up the gorge and crush the guerrillas between them. With this plan, the police hope to wipe out the whole band of freedom fighters in one go. The manoeuvres are performed in the dead of night so as not to alert their quarry.

It is to be a dawn attack. As the sky lightens the advance begins. But the guerrillas are not to be taken totally by surprise. Sandawara sits by the pool brooding over his eternal plans. He looks towards the cliff tops and his keen eyes detect, silhouetted against the lightening eastern sky, the hated shapes of clothed men. He hastily fires twice to alert his men. They leap up. Dark bodies move about the pool, then disappear. The freedom fighters have taken to the caves. Sandawara loves caves and has explored every rockhole in his earth.

Unopposed the police party reunites and converges on the cave mouths. They extend in a semi-circle before them. The guerrillas begin the fight with a ragged volley. Bullets whine off rocks, hiss through leaves and skim across the once quiet water surface. Every now and then Ellewara's gun booms out in a lethal volley of slugs which lash the trees and shower leaves and twigs on to the invading party. A man shrieks as a wire cartridge tears away his head.

Ellewara enjoys himself, even though he is running low on ammunition. He relishes the vicious kick of the butt against his strong shoulder as both barrels discharge their thunder at the hated enemy. He laughs aloud at the sound of the harmless smacks of lead slugs flattening on the cliff face above him. Close by he recognises the throaty bark of Captain's Schneider and the sharp reports of Sandawara's lighter Winchester. Ellewara loves fighting and the constant boom and crackle of gunfire. With a savage grimace he seeks a target. A hat sticks up from behind a boulder. He lets go with both barrels and the hat and part of the limestone explodes away. A strangled shout is heard. He cranes his neck to glimpse another target. A bullet zips past his face to ricochet off the back cave wall and past his head. He jerks his head in and lies low. A minute and he risks raising his face again in quest for a target. Another bullet splatters near him. Someone has him zeroed in. He curses as he lies with his face flat on the stone floor.

The morning arrives to fling its strong light over the battlefield. Ellewara, for the first time, looks around his cave and is angered to find that it is only a shallow hole in the rock. Bullets begin ricocheting all around him and he curses the trap in which he finds himself. It will be only a matter of time before he is hit by the whining metal. He must get out of the hole and into a better position – to Sandawara's cave. He knows these holes like no one else and from where he shelters there will be a line of retreat.

A bullet zips into the cave and Ellewara takes a chance. He leaps out and bounds for the cave of his leader. Just a metre from it and he has not been hit. As he dives for the entrance, his luck gives out. A slug takes him in the back. He slumps forward and is pulled to safety by Sandawara.

The leader crouches in the gloom in the main cave and coolly directs the fire of his men. The vicious splattering of the slugs all around and the whine as they glance off the stone walls does not affect him. He fires again and again at any target he can glimpse among the mass of rocks, water, trees and bushes outside in the vivid light. He curses as he realises that there is one great fault in the cave mouth. It is small and right at the base of the cliff. He and his men have only a few metres for a field of fire whereas the enemy is spread across a front of a hundred or so metres and can direct a withering fire at the cave mouth from all angles and from secure positions that cannot be reached by return fire from the cave. Aware of this and unable to overcome the disadvantage he begins to think of retreat as the steady rattle of small arms' fire intensifies from all sides. He notes how the bullets coming directly from in front often hit the roof of the caves and glance downwards, those from the right are more dangerous – they hit the left wall and ricochet off at any angle, the slugs from the left do the same in reverse. Sooner or later he realises, he and his men must be wounded. It is only a matter of time.

The first serious casualty, Ellewara, finally recovers enough to crawl down the dark passageway leading under the range to safety. Sandawara has begun to consider seriously the retreat with the sending away of the wounded. Ellewara's woman, Wandara helps her injured man along the twisting passage. He groans as he forces his badly wounded body to crawl to safety.

Sandawara urges his men to keep up a steady rate of fire. Suddenly beside him Lillewara falls back wounded. Female comrades pull him away from the cave mouth. His leader looks at him. A heavy slug has ripped along the side of his head neatly slicing the flesh from the bone. Sandawara orders him to retreat, but the warrior, wiping the blood from his face, takes his position again. He wants revenge.

At last the inevitable happens. The leader himself is hit. A direct smashing blow sends him lurching back down on to the cave floor. A bullet has thudded into his shoulder and ploughed out under the lower breastbone. Within a minute he is back at his position. His men breathe in relief.

One by one the members of the guerrilla force are wounded and move back into the cave. The leader orders the retreat to begin while he remains at his post. If only the white men would rush the cave, then he could deal them a smashing blow. But the besiegers are content to lie low and keep up their fire. Again he is wounded. He shivers and gasps, lets fall his rifle and tumbles back on to the cave floor. He clutches his side. From between his fingers blood begins to flow. Still he nods to the faithful Captain to hand him his rifle. Captain pretends not to see and turns to the cave mouth. A woman comes up to him with a handful of mud which she plasters over the gaping wound. The bleeding stops. Captain comes and helps him to his feet. A general retreat begins into the depths of the earth.

The small group of guerrillas creeps into the safety of their earth. The only sound is the faint slap of their bare feet on rock and soft moans from the wounded. They carry their unconscious leader with them. They have no torches and must feel their way through the pitch darkness. The roof rises and falls. Sometimes it soars far above their heads while in other stretches they must crawl, dragging the wounded along the rock floor. In places water, dank and almost icy, chills their feet. Deeper they creep into the darkness which is the home of, they hope, friendly spirits. Hands feel out the way and they begin to hurry as the rifle fire behind them tapers off. They slow as it begins to roar again. Their hands must feel for sudden turns in the passageway and their feet must stretch out and test the route for deep pits. Sandawara gives a low moan and regains consciousness. He insists on getting to his feet and leading the retreat. His wound begins to bleed and his blood joins the dampness of the cave floor, but he presses his spent force on at a quicker pace towards safety.

Behind him, in front of the empty cave the police patrol keeps up a heavy fire. Eventually they realise that there has been no answering fire for some time.

'Eaglehawk, him done in,' an excited Queensland 'boy' shouts out, scrambling to his feet and racing to the cave mouth. The police watch as he reaches it and looks inside. Finding it empty, he begins to dance excitedly. Warily the rest of the patrol join him. On examining the caves they find great pools of blood where Sandawara and his main body of men have fought. They conclude that the ex-policeboy has been wounded along with a lot of his followers. They hope that the blighter is near death. Later on, with the capture of Terawara, they will come to believe that the outlaw is indeed dead. They will relax until he rises to strike again.

EIGHT

NAMING DAY

Alan's intense eyes move over his followers sitting before him in the crashpad. He stands posing in front of the painting of Sandawara, feeling more and more like the great leader. His bright eyes flicker from face to face of his comrades. They are ready and eager to follow him. He will lead them from victory to victory and, like Sandawara, he'll leave nothing to chance. Every step will be planned carefully to fit into an overall plan.

'Right, kids,' he calls, flashing his grin to claim their attention. 'We've come together to do a little planning; but before that, I've decided that we should drop our white fellow names and have Nungar names.' He glances from face to face and detects no reaction, for or against. He hurries on: 'From now on I'll be known as *Sandawara*. I've told you about him and how he fought the white man to a standstill up north. We're just like him and his men and women. His struggle is now our struggle. Sue is to be *Kangawara*. She's out now looking over,' he laughs, 'the scene of the crime. You, Tom,' Alan stares at the gloomy man who can think of nothing but impending doom, 'your name from now on is *Captain*.'

'*Captain*, that's a funny name for a Nungar,' Tom breaks in, protesting. 'It's just like Tom. What's the difference?'

'Captain was a foreigner from South Australia,' Sandawara explains, patiently. 'The white fellows took him away from his land and up north, but he became one of the local people. Everyone knew him as Captain. He was Sandawara's friend, his right hand man and a true freedom fighter. It fits you because you went east for a long time.'

'Yeah,' Tom replies, vaguely alarmed at being different from the others. Why should a foreign name be stuck on him when the others have Nungar names? Just his luck!

The leader goes on: 'You, Greg, you'll be called *Ellewara*. He was a great man, the one who came before Sandawara. It was him that got the tracker to take up arms against the invaders. You are like him in lots of ways.'

'*Ellewara, Ellewara*,' Greg repeats to himself, learning his new name. He wonders how it'll go over when he forms his band, or rather becomes a drummer in a group. It has a good sound to it, like a funky disco beat.

'Now you, Rob,' he looks at the cook who's wondering what to make for the evening meal. Rob smiles nervously at Rita as he waits to be renamed.

'You'll be known as *Lillewara*. He was a good fighter and served Sandawara bravely.'

'Hi, Lillewara,' Rita whispers softly to him, squeezing his arm.

'Rita, you'll be *Wawollu*, Lillewara's woman. She looked after her man and tended his wounds. She fought by his side and was wounded trying to rescue him from certain death.'

'What happened to him then?' Tom demands.

'He was badly wounded and ended up in a concentration camp the invaders had built on Rottnest Island. But that doesn't matter. We learn from the mistakes of the past. The revolution goes forward. The bodies of the past martyrs form the barricade behind which we fight and from which we advance.'

Sandawara sounds as if he's quoting and Tom mutters under his breath: 'Commy rubbish, the only place we'll advance to is Freeo Prison.' He wonders what happened to Captain and is afraid to ask. Suddenly, he realises there might be worse things in life than jail, or are there? – death might be the best end he could hope for.

'Tom, I mean, Captain,' Sandawara breaks into the mesh of his gloomy thoughts. 'The old Captain had a brave woman named *Terawara*. Sally is to be her. Sally, you're Terawara. Captain'll take care of you and you'll take care of Captain.'

The renamed teenybopper looks at the haggard, woebegone Captain and doesn't like it one bit. He's far too old for her and far too gloomy. No fun at all! Tom flashes a glance at the little girl and shudders. He doesn't want a sister.

'You Jane, you're *Wandara*, Ellewara's woman.'

Ellewara grins in relief, he likes the kid and'll take care of her. The girl looks at Muscles and smiles across at him. She, too, likes the choice, for one day he'll be the drummer in a band. Hasn't he told her so! She looks at Terawara and feels sorry for her. That Tom, no, that Captain is too old and smells of stale wine.

The side gate slams and the repaired door thuds, opens and closes with a bang. Kangawara rushes in from casing the bank. She comes to

Sandawara's side and he explains how he's just renamed his followers and paired them off. The girl nods in agreement.

'Sandawara, I've checked out the bank. I opened a savings account so I could spend some time in there without anyone becoming suspicious. It looks good, that is if you still want to go through with it.'

'We're going to hit it the day before election day,' the leader grins. 'No one'll be expecting it. Now we've got the guns and ammo, the sooner we do it the better. What's the scene like?'

The two teenyboppers stare at one another in happiness. Things are really starting to hum. They're going to be in a real holdup with guns and everything. Captain sinks further into the mud of his soul. Maybe he should cop out? He feels the eyes of Kangawara on him and straightens up a little. Why couldn't he have been given her instead of the skinny kid?

'Inside, it's all just one big room,' the breathless, excited voice of Kangawara details. 'They have those cameras, but seeing we're going to be wearing masks, we don't have to worry about them. The vault's at the back and there's a back door to the place. It's kept bolted from the inside, but not locked. I saw one of the tellers go through it and he didn't use a key, just snipped the bolt back. After, I went around to the back. An alley goes down the side of the building and right through into the next street. Behind the bank is a yard they use for parking. The door opens on to this. Across the street, a few metres up, is another lane. This goes right through the block and comes out near here. I followed it through.'

'That'll be no good to us,' Sandawara breaks in. 'It'll lead them right back to us, if we take it. The alley beside the bank seems the best escape route. I think, I know it. It enters into the street just across from a park with a lot of cars parked around it. Greg, I mean Ellewara, can wire one and we can exchange vehicles there. After that, Captain can drive the other car into an automatic car wash. That'll give it a good clean and with all the slogans off, it'll look completely different. Of course, we'll have false number plates on. Remove them and we're home.'

Captain jerks wide awake. He doesn't know all of the plan, but his part in it seems crazy. Back east, he's rapped with bank robbers and knows how to go about such a job. 'Hey, wait one moment,' he calls out. 'The plan, what I know of it, might be O.K., but that part about using our own vehicle from the beginning and switching to a stolen one is stupid. It should be the other way round. Guys work all day and park their cars all day. We pick up one of them. Get it in the morning and have our own car parked at the park for a getaway vehicle. That way we won't have to take any chances on being traced. We'll have false plates on it and change them before we get back here. I think this way is better.'

'Yeah, so do I,' Sandawara says, smiling at Captain and even Kangawara smiles at him. He feels a little better. If he has to be part of this thing, he just better make sure that nothing goes wrong. A small amount of optimism creeps into his heart. With careful planning added to Alan's (no, Sandawara's) audacity, it just might come off. He'll check the plan over with the leader and see the place for himself.

Wawollu gets up and goes to the kitchen to make coffee. She rushes in and stops in dismay. Ron stands in the middle of the room holding a tin of Ovaltine. She wonders if he's heard anything.

Ron leers at her and holds out the can. 'Got a little something for you. I've had a few good feeds here, now I'm paying back a little.'

The girl bustles about filling the kettle and putting it on to boil, getting out the coffee jar, milk and sugar. If she stops a moment, she finds the man breathing down her neck.

'What've you been yakking about in there?' the nut asks, the great beak of his nose rising to sniff the air for information.

'Nothing much, just the usual yakka,' Wawollu replies, wishing for Rob to come to her aid.

'Those little kids are back, aren't they?' the man sneers.

'Yeah, we went to the Aboriginal Legal Service and got help to get them out,' she lies.

'Strange they let them go just like that,' the man persists.

'Things have changed,' Wawollu replies.

'Yeah, they sure have,' Ron answers with a leer. 'I can feel it in the air. There's real strange vibes about this place, real strange. Where's the wog?'

'He's staying with his family for a while.'

'Why did he leave? Didn't he like what's happening in this pad, eh?'

'No, you know he goes home once in a while, every now and again,' the nervous girl says, stumbling in her efforts to find some plausible lies to throw at the man who's always frightened her.

'The police were here, the other night – what'd they want?'

'Just a mistake, they thought we had drugs or something like that, but we didn't. Then they thought the kids were runaways, but they weren't.'

'Perhaps that Gary put them on to you? You know, he doesn't like having you lot staying in his pad.'

'No, he wouldn't do a thing like that. He ended up sleeping under a hedge that night.'

'You know those wogs, that was his way of covering up. He's a copper's nark, if I've ever seen one.'

'No, he isn't, he's all right.'

'He wants you lot out of his place.'

'No, we pay all the rent now.'

The water starts boiling and the girl spoons coffee into the mugs.

'Hey, how about a little love making?' the creep asks straight out. 'You know, I might be getting on, but I can still keep it up for hours. I like doing it real slow too!'

The girl glances at his face. The glint of his sunglasses and the leer contorting his lips sends shivers through her body. 'If you want love, there's one of those massage places just a few blocks away,' she nervously tells him.

'Just been to one. Got a hand job, but it ain't like the real thing.'

'Got to take this coffee into the others. You coming in?' the girl hurriedly replies.

'No, got to go,' and he vanishes.

Wawollu rushes into the next room to tell the others that Ron has been in the kitchen and may have listened to what they've been saying. Sandawara advises them to be very careful when the nut is around. 'He's good training in learning to shut up,' he tells them and adds: 'Just remember the enemy is always spying on us and that we have to be always on guard.'

II

Sandawara gulps his coffee down, then rushes off to find masks for the job. Ellewara takes the girls to watch him work on the car while Captain stays in the room to talk to Kangawara. In the kitchen, Wawollu and Lillewara fuck and try out their new names. Escaping from Wawollu, the cook opens the new book of recipes his girl friend has ripped off and tries to find a good dish for the night meal. Wawollu refuses to be forgotten and pesters him until her demands and his sensations coincide.

Captain sits next to Kangawara and tries to get the job into clear focus. The girl is happy that the man is showing some interest and tries to answer all his questions. The man knows how it should go and wants to protect his neck as much as possible. He tells the girl that Sandawara is too speedy and young to plan in detail and goes over the scene with her.

He moves closer to Kangawara as he talks. 'What shops are nearby?' he asks her, while becoming conscious of the nearness of her body.

'Oh, you know. There's that big pub on the corner, a coffee bar next to it, an opportunity shop, then comes the lane and the bank, beside it is a used furniture store.'

'What's across the street?' Captain asks, his mind only half on the question.

'Just a cafe and a few old houses.'

'Seems O.K.' He glances at the girl's breasts, before going on. 'I remember it now. The lane does go right through to the park. At night the police patrol it. Remember one time I got pissed and flaked out there. Woke up with the light of a flash jabbing into my eyes. They were nice, only ordered me to get the hell out of there.' Bored with the scene and watching the rise and fall of her breasts, he changes the subject: 'What do you think of this name change thing?'

'I like it. I feel more of a special group now, before it felt like just a bunch of kids talking big, now it's different. Alan, I mean Sandawara, really gets some good ideas. I have to get used to being Kangawara now instead of Sue. You know, I have to be that inside.'

'Yeah, but I ain't so hot over Captain. God, that kid and his ideas. Just because someone from South Aussie had that name up north is no reason why I have to have it.'

'But it's historical, you know, part of Nungar history. Captain was a brave soldier in the forces of resistance against the white invaders.'

'Oh, what bullshit, you've been talking to Sandawara too much. He got all his ideas from a white man anyway. Commy ideas and a kiddie mind go well together. He's all mixed up.'

'You're the one who's mixed up, not him,' the girl retorts.

'Maybe, maybe,' Captain grates out, 'but I've seen too much and know to much even to think of pretending to be some sort of freedom fighter. Who cares who runs this country as long as the hotels stay open to a decent hour. That's freedom for me, I don't want any other.'

'Yeah, yeah,' Kangawara mocks him. 'You're beginning to sound like a top forty number which has been around too long. Give it a rest, man. Anyway, we're not into this thing for ourselves. We want to open a youth hostel to help our people.'

'That's an old number too,' Captain almost snarls, his eyes on her breasts fluttering in her excitement. 'Anyway, I'm too old to be a kid. I'll go through with the job, just to show you that I'm no coward, then I'm splitting.'

Suddenly the girl begins to feel for her mixed-up brother and says softly: 'Oh Captain, if only you'd get yourself together, you'd really be an asset in our movement. It's so easy being negative and against everything, so hard to get out and fight for what you want. Just think of the old Captain, he never gave in to the forces of oppression.'

'Another thing,' Captain exclaims, veering away from the subject which threatens to overcome him, 'what about that skinny little kid Sandawara's coupled me with – what am I to do with her?'

'You have to look after her, take care of her just as she has to do the same for you. You're comrades in arms.'

'Oh damn,' Captain almost shouts, not understanding anything anymore. 'Everything's crazy, she doesn't even like me. This place is becoming worse than Ron.'

'Times have changed and ways of living have to change,' the girl echoes. 'Why don't you make the effort to get to know her. You haven't spoken a word to her since she's been here. She's as much a part of this group as you are. Sandawara says that we must start to learn to live together, to be one family and take care of each other just as the Nungars did in the old days.'

'You've learnt it all off by heart, haven't you?' Captain answers, then slides away from any seriousness. 'Besides she's just a kid. Sandawara's age. Why didn't he couple himself off with her? You're older and more my type,' he finishes, lowering his voice. He brushes her thigh, then her breasts. He attempts to kiss her, but the girl pushes him away.

'Not that again,' Kangawara groans, moving away from him. 'We always come to this and I'm sick of it.'

'Maybe you are, but I ain't. Why don't we get it on and maybe I can give my mind to the revolution?'

'Oh stop bugging me and making fun of everything,' Kangawara hisses. 'You know sometimes when you're sober I like you, but when you're drunk and nasty, I can't stand you. I don't like drunks. Alcohol has caused us too much trouble in the past and even now when I take a walk along the streets I can see the suffering it's causing.'

'Yeah, well you just take a walk along some of the streets tonight and you'll see some of that suffering called Captain lately Tom,' the man growls at her.

'Where's your self respect and Nungar respect?' Kangawara demands, her voice rising shrilly.

'I lost that a long time ago,' Captain replies. 'I was born with a stone around my neck. I'm used to it, it keeps my eyes on the ground looking for butts. I ain't got any self respect. None of us has,' he shouts out, suddenly finding himself in a position he doesn't like being in.

'We can create our own self respect,' the girl replies in a calm voice, knowing that once again she's broken through to Captain. 'Look what Sandawara's doing. He's not lying in some gutter bemoaning his fate and knowing that everyone despises him. He's up and doing something.'

'That kid'll end up in Freeo,' Captain declares, trying not to feel or care. He wants a drink – bad!

But even on the subject of jail, the girl is becoming practical: 'I've talked to a lot of people who've been inside. Jail ain't nothing much. If Sandawara went inside, he'd just start organising the people there. There's a hell of a lot of Nungars there and no one's doing a thing for them.'

'Good for him,' the thirsty Captain says, trying to hide his fear of being locked up. His terror rises like bile in his throat. 'Good for him,' he repeats, then suddenly words fall from his mouth. 'You know some people do it hard; some people don't like being like a caged animal; it drives some men out of their minds. It's worse than death,' he shouts. in despair. He needs a bottle of wine. 'I'm off to check out the scene,' he tells the girl and gets to his feet.

The girl, with tears in her eyes, watches him leave. Some of his terror and pain has been shared with her and she understands him a little more.

III

There's a wine bar in Beaufort Street which caters for the Nungars. For ten cents you can get a tiny glass of raw wine (red or white) to down. Of course it's owned by a white man. There, Captain sits slumped at the bar twirling a drop or two of red at the bottom of his midget glass. He's been to the scene of the crime and found it more or less as Kangawara has described. Now, drunk, he waits for closing time. The bar's deserted except for a Nungar woman. She smiles at him and he buys her a glass of wine. Side by side they sit and sip in silence.

'Don't like this joint much,' the woman talks. 'These itty bitty glasses are thimbles, cheaper to buy a bottle, then you can go and relax somewhere quiet and drink it.'

'Yeah,' Captain agrees, 'that's a fact. These white fellows make a mint out of us.'

'That they do,' the woman replies, watching Captain as he beckons for their glasses to be refilled.

They sip on. Nothing is happening. Captain staggers to the juke box and tries to make out the record list. Charley Pride and Slim Dusty. He fumbles in his pockets, but can't find a twenty cent coin. He meanders back to the bar.

'Don't think I've seen you in here before,' the woman says.

'Too classy for me,' the man smiles without mirth. 'I get around a lot and go to this pub and that pub, to this park and that park. I come in here sometimes. Our times have never crossed before, that's all.'

'What's your name?' the woman asks, wondering what part of the state he's from.

He turns to her and finds that she reminds him of his mother, long gone, lost or died when he was east. 'Captain,' he finally answers.

'That's a real old name,' the woman says, wondering if he's lying. 'Remember they used to give us names like that in the old days. Captain and Pigeon, Blackie and Nigger, King Billy – names like that. My name's Mary, good Catholic name. Named after a farmer's daughter, I am.'

'Yeah,' Captain replies. 'I'm named after a man up north near Derby. He was a strong bloke, he was.'

'You from up that way? I'm from Katanning, one of the Morisses.'

'Heard of them. Isn't one of them playing football for East Perth.'

'Yeah, Jack, one of my cousins.'

'You want to get your glass topped up again?'

'No, don't like this stuff. Too much of it and you wake up with the heebie jeebies. It's almost on dosing time, too. Got enough money for a couple of bottles? Can get them for a dollar twenty here.'

The man fumbles through his pockets and pulls out a crumbled two dollar bill. 'Only got this,' he slurs out.

'Well, I got forty cents. Added to that it makes enough. We get them and go some place and enjoy them. We can have a bit of a good time if things turn out right.'

'Are there any good times left?' the drunken Captain mutters, taking up the two bottles and stumbling out after the woman. She guides him along a street running parallel to the railway tracks. She goes down alongside a derelict house and into a shed in the backyard. After Captain enters she carefully closes the door and strikes a match to light a piece of rag hanging out of a small tin filled with kerosene. In the flickering smoky flame, the man makes out a dirty mattress crumbled along one wall and filling most of the floor space. He slumps on it and opens one of the bottles. He takes a swig of the sweet sherry and passes it to the woman. Back and forth the bottle goes.

Soft, hesitant sounds at the door and it edges open to admit a man who slithers through. He carefully shuts the door before turning to them.

'Hello Mary,' his soft voice says. 'Got any wine?'

'Yeah, this fellow here, name's Captain, he helped me to get a bottle. Here have a swig.'

The black man grunts, clutches the bottle and drains it in one swallow. Wiping his mouth, he sprawls on the mattress and looks at Captain. 'You ain't no Captain, you're that Tom bloke I was drinking with down at the Grove.'

'I've changed my name,' Captain slurs out.

'Well, I suppose a man's got a right to change his name if he wants to just as he's got a right to change his strides,' the man says, introducing himself as Bill Sykes. 'You got another bottle there?' he says, picking it up. He uncorks it and takes a swig. Captain takes it from him, takes a long swallow and passes it to Mary.

'Where'd you meet Mary?' Bill Sykes asks Captain.

'At the wine bar.'

'Never go there. Can't get a big enough swallow from one of those thimbles. Bloke needs to drink out of a bottle to drown his thirst.'

He applies actions to his words and upends the bottle. Captain watches the wine vanishing and grabs for the bottle.

'Me and Mary live here,' Bill says. 'She's my woman. She's from Katanning way; I'm from Geraldton.'

'Been up there,' Captain replies. 'You know the Coves?'

'Yeah, related to them on my mother's side. Got to go and let out some of the wine. Be right back. Think, I've got a half flagon stashed somewhere outside. See if I can find it.'

Bill Sykes gets up and slips out of the door. Captain finishes off the last few drops in the bottle and waits for the man to return. Minutes go by. He decides that the man isn't coming back and reaches for the woman. He pulls her to him, tasting the sweet wine taste of her lips. She doesn't mind, but her returning man does.

'What're you doing with my woman? Just go outside for a minute and come back to find you all over her. She's my woman, she is!'

'Oh hell,' Captain exclaims and tries to lie his way out of it: 'Didn't mean anything by it. Just kissing her goodbye, she helped to buy the wine, got to be on my way now.'

The man scowls at Captain as he lurches to his feet. 'See you around,' he says as he staggers out of the shed. 'Fuck it,' he declares at the night as he stumbles towards the back of the house. Falling forward, he catches himself against a door. Automatically he tries the handle. It turns. He stumbles through the opening into darkness and wanders from bare dusty room to bare dusty room, feeling his way. He can't see a thing, except when he enters a front room where the light from a street lamp pushes through a window. He comes against a closed door and pushes against it. A candle flutters inside and a man sits on a dirty mattress surrounded by what Captain takes to be rags. He staggers forward and is startled to see the man's eyes glinting up at him.

'Hi Ron,' he slurs, falling on the mattress next to the man. 'You got any wine?'

The Beaufort Street nut takes a while to answer. He's been surprised in one of his lairs and feels invaded. Finally, at last, seeing that Tom isn't going to go away, he makes the best of an awkward situation and picks up a half filled flagon of red wine and passes it across.

'Man, I need this,' Captain says, gulping it down. 'You met that black bloke out the back? He caught me kissing his woman. I thought he was going to do me.'

'Yeah,' Ron replies with a nasty grin, 'I borrowed this wine off him. He'll never miss it. Why'd you go after that old Mary when you got those two young'uns back at Gary's?'

'I don't go for those kids,' Captain replies. 'They're all skin and bone.'

Ron leers: 'I know what they're like. Nice and tight.'

'Maybe, maybe, you're the expert,' Captain answers, raising the flagon to his lips and spilling the wine down over the front of his shirt. He reaches for one of the rags and finds that it's a pair of women's panties. He picks up another rag and finds that it's a petticoat.

'What've you been doing, collecting bits and pieces from clothes lines?' he. asks, then adds: 'Don't answer, I don't want to know, I've got problems of my own. Too many problems, what with Sandawara and his carryons. He's a right one, he is.'

'Who's this Sandawara?' Ron demands, leaning forward ready to soak up the info.

'Oh, I mean Alan,' Captain answers, deciding not to tell the man about the name changes. Somehow it's not the thing to do. He drinks some more wine. 'Well, I got problems, man. I should cut off up north.'

'Why, Tom, they cross you off the dole?' Ron asks, friendly-like, but with a sneer.

Captain is too drunk to notice the man's attitude towards him. 'No, that's all right, only other things bug me, things that are happening at the pad.'

'What things?' the Beaufort Street nut asks eagerly, then to cover up adds: 'Those little girls not giving you any? Give them a little taste of wine and you'll get all you want.'

'Who cares about them? There's worse things happening, like guns and things.'

'Is that why Gary left?' Ron asks casually, reaching for the flagon, taking a sip, then passing it back to Captain. He watches him take a long pull. Patience and a little more wine will get everything from him.

'You know,' the man says, leaning over and grabbing Ron's sleeve, 'I can talk to you, right? I never harmed you in any way. I never harm anyone in any way. All I want is a drink now and again and the feel of a woman when I can get it without hurting anyone. I'm harmless, but I'm going to end up in a jail for robbing a bank. Me, robbing a bank. I have to, I can't get out of it, I'm no coward, could never hold my head up again if I backed out, but I don't want to go to jail ...' and his voice falls into the Nungar mumble and Ron strains his ears to make out an occasional word. In an effort to get the man coherent again, he presses the flagon into his hands. Captain takes a swig and comes out of the defensive mumble to confess: 'You know I'm a graduate of Greystone, I did time in the east? Got put away for smashing into a pub for a lousy carton of beer. A pig tar came snorting along. I got six months. God, I hate that place. I can't stand being locked up. I go crazy ...' his voice falls into a mumble while Ron files the information for future use. He brings Captain back to the present by saying: 'But you're clean in Perth. You're not in trouble, are you? I know that you've been in for the night now and again for being drunk, but that's all!'

'That's right, I keep out of trouble, but now trouble's arrived on my doorstep. It's waiting to greet me now. That stupid Sandawara wants to rob a bank and the others want to, too. It's crazy, they've got guns and are all ready to go tomorrow. I'm trapped in it and I don't want to do it. Man, I'll go crazy in jail. I can't stand it.' He grabs the flagon and upends it over his mouth. He sucks at it seeking oblivion.

'What bank?' Ron dares to ask, not expecting an answer, but hoping for one.

'You know that one in Oxford Street near the pub? We're going to hit it right on closing time. We might pull it off too,' he adds wistfully, hopefully. 'We just might at that.'

Suddenly he lurches back against the wall, out like a light. Ron calls his name a few times, but gets not a sign of an answer. Then he begins to laugh his laugh: 'Heh, heh, heh, heh.' Now he's got them; now he'll have his revenge against all the boongs for what they have done to him.

NINE

DAY OF WRATH

Ron slinks along under the hot summer sun. The man slinks, not from shadow to shadow, but from light patch to light patch on the shady side of the road. He seems to be daring the sun to puncture through his thick clothing and hat. The nut's a dark shade fighting the sun and even winning. Ron doesn't sweat – though he exudes a cold-sweat dampness.

His trenchcoat is tightly belted about his body, the coat collar huddles over his ears and almost touches the pulled down brim of his hat. His mirror sunglasses reflect the dazzling streets and camouflage his leer – of revenge about to be fulfilled, of gloating satisfaction, of pretence, of unease and guilt. A cackle slithers from his mind and rattles out into the world as a heh, heh, heh, heh. The sounds rise to a crescendo and trail off into a fit of coughing which brings up a glob of phlegm to be ejected into the day.

The man circles the fuzzy shadow of an almost leafless tree and blends with it as he bends over to check out a litter bin. He emerges into the reality of the white-hot streets before his objective – the police station. 'Heh, heh, heh, heh,' his cackle oozes out and stops as a teenage girl in cunt tight jeans wriggles past. What a creep, she thinks, suddenly conscious of the provocativeness of her body and attire. She shudders, feeling creepy-crawly things inching and itching over her back. The girl wants to glance back to see if the man is following her. She manages to control herself – after all it is broad daylight – until she is almost at a turn off. She flings one whitefaced glance over a frightened shoulder before escaping around the corner.

Even then, she feels threatened. Her steps speed up and so does the wriggling of her behind. Every few steps she flings scared eyes around. Each time, the girl breathes in relief at seeing no one. But she can almost swear that someone is close on her heels breathing down her neck. 'What a creep,' she whispers, darting a glance behind her. In relief she enters her work place.

But this morning the creep has other things to be excited about. After following the girl for a few steps, hesitating, then going on to the corner to look after her, he has returned to his objective and entered. Avoiding all contact with underlings by a process of not being seen, he appears in the office of the two detectives now facing a day shift of stultifying boredom.

Detective Collins is typing up a report. A master of the two-finger technique of speed typing, he can rattle off a report on the old Remington at forty words a minute. But today the heat and the lack of a crime wave added to a half dozen pots of beer (Emu Bitter of course, the best in the west if you're not a Swan Lager man) has slowed him down to six words and six mistakes a minute.

'Some bloody bloke punching up his old woman. Probably the bag asked for it,' he growls out to his mate, Kelly, who somnolent through heat, boredom and beer (Swan Lager, the best on earth), has taken to executing the lazy flies, walking and crawling and flip-flopping through the air. He aims the nozzle of the aerosol can of poison at one such criminal and gives the button a soft press. The lethal spray hisses out until one more insect curves from the air to the floor.

The detective's red-rimmed eyes stare at the struggle from kicking life to still death. No, only a swoon, for the fly buzzes into life and zooms up to the desk for an all-legged (or seven point) landing of love on another of its kind.

'God,' Kelly grinds out, 'what the hell is in this can that causes good Aussie flies to turn Spanish?'

In disgust, he voyeurs the fly-fucking, then gives the lovers a long, long burst. The male (i.e. the one on top) noticeably increases his rhythm and the female (the one on the bottom) appears to reciprocate. In anger, the detective raises one meaty hand and slams it down on the desk top. The union, with a little help from the human, becomes truly one. Never to be separated, ever again, the two flies lie squashed in death.

'Bloody disgusting,' Kelly growls, turning his slow anger on his partner's laboured tap-tap, stop, tap-tap on the cursed machine which he has found beyond his power to master.

He looks up from the mess on his desk and gives a start – an exaggerated start: anything which relieves his ennui is welcome – as he sees the fruitcake standing at the door and examining the room. Almost gleefully, Kelly's eyes harden and his body reshapes itself into that of the aggressive detective.

'Who the bloody hell let you in?' he roars out.

Collins, not be outdone, heaves himself to his feet (he can't manage a leap) and, with not quite the speed of his favourite television cop, lumbers the few steps to the desk. He perches on a corner. A shoulder holster would have made him more impressive, but unfortunately outdated rules state that a gun must be signed out and the purpose stated. One day (and that day soon) both detectives know the rule will go the way of all bad laws and then they'll be able to lounge around like true detectives do.

Now weaponless, they seek to awe by other means. With eyes of steel, they try to dominate the nut in front of them. His defences are strong. The mirrors of his eyes make them feel a little foolish, but like all good actors, they continue to play out their roles.

'All right, what do you want this time? Out with it,' Kelly shouts.

Collins adopts the soft approach. 'Well Ron, you were right about those two little kids being there – but you still had us expecting drugs, and there weren't any. What have you brought us this time?' Collins smiles, wishing he could take those damn sunglasses and ram them down the nut's throat.

'And it better be something good,' Kelly menaces, eyeing distastefully, not Ron, but his partner wiping off the fly corpses with a piece of blotting paper. 'Well, what?' he snarls at the nut, still not looking at him. He vows to put this fruitcake away one day for a long stretch, info or no info, crime or no crime.

Ron stands studying Collins' method of concealing his partner's crime. He looks at him over the top of his sunglasses and for an instant their eyes meet. The detective glances away, not wanting to share anything with such a lunatic.

Ron at last appears directly in front of the desk. He begins muttering away. The two detectives shout: 'Speak up!' More mutters which gradually clear into words.

Slowly and hesitatingly, with many patches of incomprehensibility, circumlocutions and asides about getting his own back mixed in with what had been done to those poor little girls, the story of the bank job begins to take shape.

The cops every now and again pick up a detail, examine it and cast it aside:

'You say guns, what? – pistols?'

'Rifles,' embroiders Ron who doesn't know.

'How many?'

'Well, you know that Greg is a real bad one. He'll kill someone one of these days and he hates cops. Who knows what foul things, they done to those poor little girls. Last time I saw my sister, she was that age. They said I did things to that poor little tyke. Me, I never touched her!' He leers at the detectives and they forget about rifles and bank robbers. They try to recall any unsolved cases of child molesting.

'They might have a dozen rifles,' Ron swings back.

'What about ammo?' Kelly growls.

'And they got it all planned out – down to the last detail. You know just before the bank closes, they come in. They got guns and all. Rifles and lots of bullets. Knives too ...'

'But they're just kids,' Collins breaks in through the mumbling 'They're just having you on.'

'You know what kids are like,' Ron rattles on. 'They do anything these days. I knew this little girl ...' and his mutterings turn into gibberish. The words pushing through his leer lose all shape and substance.

The two cops exchange glances and yawns. The welcome diversion has become part of the general tedium of the afternoon. Collins, being the gentleman this time around, at last mildly says: 'Well, thank you Ron, you've given us all the facts and we'll look into it.'

'You better,' the nut replies. 'It's your chance to make the headlines.'

'That's enough,' Collins shouts, his kind guy image vanishing. 'Now get out before we lock you up and throw away the key, you bloody pervert.'

'They've got guns,' Ron quietly says.

'Yeah, yeah,' Kelly says with a hard laugh.

'We've got all the facts and we'll look into it,' the recovered Collins adds, again practising his police good public relations image.

'And if you don't hurry, it'll be all over,' the nut states, then changes the subject and aims his words at Collins who appears to be the soft touch today. 'Now Inspector, how about a dollar for a meal? You know how hard it is to get along on a pension these days. Prices just keep rising higher and higher. Many a day I have to go without a bite to eat.'

'Go to the Salvation Army, they'll give you something to chew on,' Collins growls out, his mask slipping again. 'Get out of here before I put you on a charge. Get out, go on, you lunatic!'

'And don't come back unless it's with something better than a cock-and-bull story,' Kelly shouts.

The cops get to their feet, ready for a bit of excitement. Ron vanishes. A little put out they stare at each other.

'Think there's anything in it?' Kelly asks Collins.

'Could be,' Collins replies to Kelly.

Both men are suddenly conscious of the boredom descending. It hovers over them like the swarm of flies. No amount of fly spray can compete with the glory of a holdup foiled all spread out in headlines instant with promotion. They decide to act on the reliable information they have received.

'Right, Collins,' Kelly snaps. 'We better draw some firearms.'

'I'll get a load of uniforms along too,' Collins snaps back.

'They better be armed too. No knowing what we'll be up against.'

Phones jangle, setting wheels in motion. Collins and Kelly prepare to go and get themselves some bank robbers.

II

Meanwhile the wouldbe robbers – not robbers, guerrilla fighters – are getting ready to strike their first blow in the fight for – unfortunately Sandawara hasn't exactly figured it out yet. He's going to liberate money for a hostel as the first step towards-self-reliance, liberty, self-determination, the ultimate creation of Nungarland? A clear policy has yet to be formulated, but they are ready to strike the first blow.

By pooling their dole money and by shop lifting they've managed to get army fatigues from a disposal store. Sandawara wears a paratrooper's camouflaged overalls and Kangawara, ever attentive to his needs, has taken them to the Nungar Women's Selfhelp Centre to unstitch, recut and sew them together again. The leader pulls the remade overalls over his jeans and shirt, then puts on high canvas jungle boots and laces them up. The youth struts about feeling a real soldier. He would have liked to wear a beret, but has decided against it. Ellewara has one on and in his khakis looks more a garage attendant than a fighter in the cause of freedom. It doesn't worry him. He's never wanted to be a soldier – only a drummer in a band. His mind is filled with lots of money and a shiny set of drums

Kangawara doesn't know how she feels in the baggy uniform. She knows that Sandawara looks dashing, but she thinks she appears either as a fringe dweller or someone on the way to a not very fashionable fancy dress party. She tries to adjust her clothing. It has been drilled into her always to 'dress decent', and the girl hates appearing like a tramp. Still Kangawara will wear what her leader tells her to wear and will follow him to hell and back. Standing before her in his pose, the youth looks every inch a leader and her heart goes out to him.

In his rumpled fatigues, Captain looks a drunk and is half drunk. His mind fills with dread over the coming job and he can't help comparing his clothing to the rough garb of a convict. The D.T.s hit him. He hallucinates around him the thick greystone walls and barred windows of Freeo jail. The vision wavers, but remains even though he swallows a bottle of red. Strangely, this sobers him up. He almost prays for the guts to walk away from the crazy mob. He doesn't need money. The dole is enough for him to drink on. Then he stares at Kangawara. Once he had thought she was a girl with common sense. He looks at Sandawara posing, and wonders why he's following such a kid. He glances around at the others. If he could cry, he would be crying, not for them but for himself. In the abyss all Captain wants to do is to drink himself senseless. But he can't, he's part of the mob and won't play a coward and pull out. He'll go through with it!

The rifles are loaded and lying on the mattresses. Sandawara makes sure that the safety catches are on. Next to them lie eight rubber masks. The two teenyboppers, looking very young and fragile in their too big clothes are wild-eyed and out of their minds with excitement. They try on the masks and try to scare each other.

'Hey, some lark, eh?' Terawara grins at Wandara. She grabs up a rifle and points it at the other girl. 'Bang, bang, you're dead,' she cries. The other girl doesn't find it funny. 'Hey, put that down, it's loaded,' she protests and makes a grab for it.

'Stop that, you kids,' Sandawara raps.

They spring apart, sit on the mattresses and wait for the next scene in this exciting drama.

In the kitchen Lillewara and. Wawollu stand together making violent love. Wawollu has discovered that baggy pants with a zipper don't have to be removed. Over-excitedly, she pushes herself against her lover, squirming and banging against him. Lillewara forgets about the sandwiches he's been making. Just as horny and elated as his girl friend, he bangs her up against the wall. Her arms hang her body about his neck and he braces himself to accept her whole weight as her legs encircle his waist. He stands still as the girl's cunt does all the work. It has a life of its own, a rhythm of its own. Both stand motionless. Tremors travel across their bodies. Lillewara feels that the life is being sucked from him. He tenses and tries to fight it. His whole body begins shaking, shuddering and the girl begins to moan deep down within her throat. The youth sinks to the ground as he begins to come. They shudder on and on. It seems that the ecstasy will never end. They moan and begin to get frightened at the strength and length of their mutual orgasm. At last, it ends leaving them shaken and spent.

'Wow,' the girl says, finding it difficult to move a finger.

'Wow,' the youth replies in a faint whisper.

'So that's what it's all about,' Wawollu whispers, her lips quivering in a smile.

Huddled together on the floor, they stay there until at last, strengthened by a kiss, they manage to get up.

'Let's finish off the sandwiches,' Lillewara says.

'Mmmm,' Wawollu replies, then gently comes against him. 'That was enough for ever.'

'Until the next time,' the youth smiles shyly, conscious of how much he loves her.

'And I love you too,' she replies as if reading his mind.

Together they start wrapping the sandwiches. Lillewara has just discovered wholemeal bread and a sandwich spread which is really delicious. He hopes the others will think so too.

'They will, they will,' the girl murmurs as she takes up the packet.

'At least the kids will,' Lillewara says. 'They eat anything.'

Wawollu gives him a last kiss, then stands back to let him walk in front of her. She watches him moving in his baggy uniform and hums the tune, 'Little Boy Lost'. She feels such a great love for her lover that in the passageway she can't help grabbing him from behind and hugging him.

Charly brushes past them. They look after him in amazement. The man has changed from the down and outer. He wears clean jeans, cowboy boots, a checked shirt and a widebrimmed hat. A silence falls as he enters the room.

'Hey man, what's happened to you?' Sandawara asks, eyeing him in disbelief.

'Where's the war?' the new Charly asks, equally astonished at their getup.

The leader begins to exude charm. Charly has got himself together and that could mean another follower.

'We're off to get the money to open our hostel,' he says with a smile.

'With those?' Charly replies, nodding at the half dozen rifles on the mattresses.

'With those,' Sandawara states. 'You want to be in on it? You're one of us. We're sick and tired of being pushed around. Now we are going to stand up for our rights and take back what's ours. Tomorrow's polling day and we're getting ready to cast the Nungar vote. Come and vote with us.'

Sandawara stands there, taut and tense, projecting his power at the man. He is the leader to right all wrongs. His followers feel the intensity, the passion radiating from him. He stands and waits for the answer which can only be 'Yes!' Kangawara gazes at him with admiration, but Charly, just up from the depths, is unmoved.

'What exactly are you going to do?' he asks.

'Rob a bank,' Sandawara states calmly. 'Rob a bank,' he exclaims passionately. 'We're going to take back what's ours. These white people took all the land and never paid anything for it. Well, we're going to collect the first instalment on that debt.' He finishes with his broad grin.

Charly shakes his head. 'Count me out. I ain't got the uniform anyway. Might make it another time.'

Sandawara accepts what he considers a copout. It is to be only the first of many blows. He is fighting a war not a battle and there will be a next time. 'That's all right,' he grins closing the matter. 'But what's happened to you?'

'Got me a job,' the man replies, 'in a pub singing Country and Western.'

'You have?' Ellewara butts in enviously. 'Got a spot for a drummer? I'll be getting my set soon and be on the lookout for gigs.'

'Don't know, maybe later,' the singer answers. 'At the moment, there's only me and a guitar working. I came to borrow Gary's guitar. Where is he?'

'Arrh he's gone away,' Ellewara tells him. He left his axe behind and you can use it.' He looks in admiration at a real musician singing for money.

Charly picks up the guitar, tunes it and begins to sing a song which makes Captain feel right at home.

Come listen all you Nungars,
Come listen to my tale
Of our poor downtrodden brothers,
Arotting there in jail.
They committed no real crime
Apart from being black;
Some don't know why they're in there
And probably will go back.

But prison's nothing special
To any Nungar I know,
'Cause the white man makes it prison
Most everyplace we go.

We'd really like to find out,
Just how to apply for bail;
But then we cannot raise it
So it's back again to jail.
That's where my story started,
And probably will end,
So don't be too downhearted
At least we don't pretend.

And prison's nothing special
To any Nungar I know,
'Cause the white man makes it prison
Most everyplace we go.

III

The stolen car has been radicalised into a vehicle of political protest. Sandawara has carefully considered the matter and concluded that the best camouflage is not a blending in but a sticking out like a sore thumb. He believes that no one seeing such a bedaubed and bedecked vehicle will have the slightest suspicion that it is a stolen car on the way to do a bank job. As usual he's right. One side of the vehicle is devoted to the Labor Party. On the doors portraits of Gough stare petulantly out with a slightly dazed expression as if he is suffering from the shock of being rejected by the Australian people. Beneath him is: SHAME SHAME SHAME. On the other side, portraits of Malcolm Fraser, the Liberal Party leader, evade the eyes. His expression can only be described as blank, but his prominent lantern jaw gives him a certain conservative strength. Beneath him flashes the slogan: TURN ON THE LIGHTS. Across the front bumper, is a sticker: 'Vote for Labor', in lower case letters, and across the back bumper in bold bright letters one that demands: A VOTE FOR THE LIBERALS. A sign in the back window has been hastily scrawled and reads: LONG LIVE SANDAWARA.

The mob admire their work before piling into the car. Ellewara is the driver. Next to him sit Sandawara then Kangawara. Captain carries out the rifles wrapped in a blanket and sticks them in the back on the floor. Wawollu has the masks in a pillow case and goes to put them on top of the rifles, but the leader calls to her: 'Hand them out, we'll put them on now.'

'You think it wise?' the gloomy Captain asks.

'Yeah, man,' the itching-to-go Sandawara grins. 'No one'll think that bank robbers'd drive through town like this. Everyone's electioneering, we're part of the show.'

The leader has been given the best mask, that of a ferocious black, unfortunately African. He tugs it on and the others follow his example. Ellewara turns into a wolfman; Kangawara into a hideous old witch; Lillewara into Frankenstein's monster, and Wawollu flashes a grin at her boyfriend as she pulls on a livid skull. They hug each other and feel weird. Meanwhile Captain has turned into Count Dracula. The pale, gaunt face fits him perfectly. He feels that he'll certainly look like that when he's finally released from prison. Wandara and Terawara become terrible twins. Both have monster masks, all buck teeth and bulging eyes. Wandara puts up her hands, hooks her fingers into claws and lunges at her friend, who retreats in mock fright.

'Right, the rest of you get into the back seat,' Sandawara commands. They scramble in. Lillewara is happy to find it such a tight squeeze that his girl friend has to sit on his knees. His girl is now able to hug and caress her lover all the way to the bank. Captain climbs into the middle and is surprised when Terawara jumps on to his lap. The other girl gets in and slams the door. The teenybopper bounces on the sad sack's knee and grins at her friend. The masks hide all expression.

'How about a last song?' Sandawara calls to Charly who is standing beside the car, his mouth gaping as he takes in the wonder of it all. 'And not like that other one either,' the leader commands. 'Give us something rousing.'

'Here's one, I just heard the other day,' the singer replies, snapping out of his bemusement. He lifts the guitar and begins:

Poor bugger me, Gurindji,
Me bin sit down this country
Long time before Lord Vestey.
Allabout land belongin' to we
O poor bugger me.
Poor bugger blackfeller this country
Long time work no wages we
Work for good old Lord Vestey.
Little bit plour, chugar and tea
For the Gurindji from Lord Vestey.
O poor bugger me.

Wolfman turns the ignition key. Slowly the overladen vehicle pulls into the street and picks up speed. Charly strums the last chords and stares after it shaking his head.

TEN

VICTORY AND DEFEAT

Noorak sits by his fire sunk in dreams of Sandawara, seeing again in vision those days when fear is in the white man and the campfires of the people buzz with the tales of their hero's exploits, of how the patrols seek him here, there and everywhere while he roams at will with his band across his earth, while he rests safely in one cave or the other, while he watches, strikes, runs and turns to strike again.

The old man's eyes reflect the flickering flames of the fire playing with the darkness and creating shape and form, illusion and reality. His eyes are motionless, unblinking, unseeing – freed, his mind can roam at will, in words and in images, over the land and into the past.

Sandawara is strange, men whisper. The white fellows call him, Eaglehawk, a bird. Birds love the sky, it is their land, but this man always seeks the secret underground places far from the sky. It is not so strange, for do not the cloud-messengers, the rain bringers love the dark secret places too? Wandjina that made the earth and everything, that made man and gave him his land on which to live. Wandjina lives in caves and gives rain to the earth which is warm and breathes, live with their breath of steam which rises to fall as rain. Wandjina is the earth and sky and everything between and, like his spirit ancestors, Sandawara loves to live close to them in the earth. Like a serpent, his line of retreat is always back into the earth and he alone knows the underground places. Those which enter the ground and stay there and his own holes which go a long, long way in to meet other tunnels until finally, at last, after many miles they turn up to come out into the clear day or soft evening light far, far away from where he had gone to earth and where the white men lie waiting in ambush, confident that they have him trapped.

Time and time again with a patrol hot on his heels, racing along before the keen eyes of the Queensland trackers, he vanishes, sometimes even on the bank of a deep pool surrounded by bush and easily searched. The police and trackers spend many hours thrashing about in the scrub and even set fire to it to drive him out, but this country is not theirs and it has taken its own to it. He cannot be found. At last, they give up, puzzled and angry and ride away from the desolation they have caused. Cursing, the white men ride back to their base, promising never to take him alive. He has outwitted them too often, far too often. But the trackers, taken far from their own earth, sit around their campfires and murmur throughout the night, creating legends of this man who is more than a man. They whisper that he creates the caves into which he descends.

And how does Sandawara escape? He swims a river, or pool to a cliff or hillside to haul himself up into a hole which covers him quietly. The hot sun quickly dries the wet imprints of his feet and hands. They search in vain while Sandawara writhes through the ground to where he has left fire-making sticks and torches of gummy bark and leaves. Igniting them, he continues on his journey until he finally emerges into the open air on a ridge-top or a tableland far from his pursuers.

The police come to hate and to fear Sandawara. They see him not as a valiant fighter to be treated with respect, but as something inhuman from the dark depths to be exterminated. After a raid when Sandawara and his men scatter to confuse pursuit, it is after him that the patrols thunder. His men joke about it and he laughs along with them. A loud laugh which suddenly clicks off. The leader cannot afford to relax. His men watch and wonder. Sandawara's eyes have grown cold, like the floors of some of his caves, like the eyes of a serpent, and his voice sounds often like a distant echo, or the roar of the bullroarer summoning men to secret ceremonies. He listens to his men and chuckles and says: 'Those white fellows really love me. They run after me all the time and how can I say "no" to them. They love me so much that they want me to be with them for ever – in a little hole in the ground with no way out. You better watch out that they don't start loving you and come chasing after you. They want you just a little now, and once they catch you, you'll never be free of them.' His voice hisses, then echoes on: 'So take care and always cover your tracks. Always be on your guard and be sure that no tracks lead towards your refuge in the earth. Never leave a mark for them to follow; never sleep with both eyes closed, or one day you'll sleep on with lead in your guts. Just remember what happened to Alinda, the moonman, and you'll never be caught unawares. Alinda wronged his wives by killing their children. They found out about it and wanted revenge. At last they caught him sleeping in his hut. Those women burnt it to the ground with him in it. How they laughed when they watched him die in great pain amid the burning logs. But he was more than a man and their laughter ceased when he came to life before their very eyes.

'That moonman began to laugh now and he changed into a thin snake which gradually flattened into a large silver ball, like a giant honeyant. It floated to the top of the trees and from there, Alinda spoke to every thing in the world. "You will all die," he declared, "and never come to life again in the same form. You women that have tried to kill me, when I have grown as round as this in the sky, will shed blood for your crime in seeking to destroy me. My home'll be in the sky so that everyone will know that I am still alive. I will die for only three days of the month and then I will come alive again and live, then die again, then live, then die and so for ever!" We are not like Alinda,' Sandawara says with a dry chuckle, 'and must take care, for once we are dead we will never be as we are now.'

His men look at one another with moist eyes. Death is ever present and as warriors they face it with a jest, but now it hits them with all its reality. They whisper that it is love of death that leads Sandawara on, that chills his eyes and makes him seek out the caves of the Wandjina. They believe that he wants to conquer not the white man, but death itself, that he wants to become a Wandjina and recreate the Law.

Around the campfires the tales are formed and merged with old myths until the trackers go in fear of meeting Sandawara. They believe that he is no longer a man, or if a man, a great mapan (shaman) who can control the forces of nature. When Sandawara disappears and is nowhere to be found, it is because he travels in the spirit land. Even the white police call him a devil and shake their heads over their failure to run him down. For over two years he has been out against the invaders and has become the hero of countless corroborees throughout the Kimberleys. Sandawara transcends tribal boundaries just like the spirit men of the beginning. He is taken to the hearts of his people and in the terrible future he will be there to give them strength.

Noorak's eyes stare right through the fire, down into the earth and into a cave – the cave of the Wandjina. The tall, broad-shouldered man with the warrior scars across his back and shoulders, huddled over a dim fire, is Sandawara. Wild eagle feathers are knotted into his hair. He broods in the home of his ancestors.

Noorak knows the cave well. It is a sacred dreaming place of his people and well hidden from the uninitiated. To enter it a man has to wade along a creek almost lost in a tangle of jungle-like bush that is alive with snakes and spirit guardians. The entrance is a narrow slit in the rock which gives into a narrow low passageway winding deep underground where finally it opens out into a wide, high chamber.

The place of the Law and the secret ceremonies. Here, Wandjina live on in essence so that men might visit them, learn their laws and walk the right paths. Here also lie the skeletons of tribal dead who have returned to the source. In this holy place, surrounded by the white bodied and haloed faces of the Wandjina, Sandawara broods over his next move in the plan to liberate his earth – the land given to him, his ancestors and successors by the creative spirits whose white faces and dark pits of eyes gaze down upon him in understanding.

He ponders on what to do. To raid a cattle station for guns and then to retreat to a secure area to train more men to handle them, and then to raid and raid until enough arms have been captured to equip all the fighting men of the tribes in the last great struggle to drive the invaders from the countryside into Derby and at last into the sea, or – he comes back to the immediate future. A simple plan, without risk, to get guns is decided on. Always, the need for arms, and always Sandawara plots to capture them. Alone, they can free his land.

II

The heavy supply waggon creaks along the Derby to Fitzroy River Crossing Road. It groans under a heavy load. Six months' rations together with arms and ammunition for the police patrol guarding the ford. Behind it, for protection, travels a cattle station waggon. Each vehicle is guarded by three well armed mounted troopers ready to blaze away at the slightest sign of trouble. The teamsters are four very apprehensive black men with six savage dogs for added safety.

Well along on the journey, they move through liberated country. On edge, the troopers constantly scan the bush on either side. Their rifles are held across their saddles, ready to be jerked u p and fired.

Strangely for them, the journey has been a lonely one with not even a glimpse of what they contemptuously refer to as 'bush niggers'. Little wonder, for the people know that the white men shoot at any black men or black women foolish enough to show themselves. Still as the invaders press on, they feel that eyes are noting their progress and this causes them to be even more jumpy. A movement in the scrub to one side of the road. Six rifles crack. That night they enjoy wallaby stew. Their uneasiness fades. Only a few more days and they'll be through.

But Sandawara receives reports of their progress. He is determined to attack them, perhaps too determined. He is over-anxious for the supplies. He needs weapons as a man needs a woman, and he'll always need guns. He must have them if there is to be a real campaign. This shapes all his thinking and causes him to take risks. Hidden beside the road, he and his men feel the dust settle on their skins as the waggons roll past. They smile grimly at the sudden firing and the instant death of an animal. They lope along after the vehicles and watch as the enemy makes camp. The plan is for a dawn attack. Half of his men will rush the camp; others will drive off the horses, and the rest will be held in reserve, ready to hasten up to support either group.

It is a good plan, but the thudding, bare feet of a small boy pounds towards them. He reaches the leader and falls, panting at his feet. Bad news: a police patrol is approaching.

'We'll fight them,' Sandawara growls, reaching for his rifle.

'But plenty, plenty white fellows come galloping here,' the boy gasps out.

Quickly Sandawara orders some of his men to disperse, to scatter far and wide. In this way he hopes to lure the patrol away, and then to regroup and smash the camp. He nods to Ellewara and Captain to withdraw with the main body of men into the nearby foothills. They are to wait there until midnight, then return. He shinnies up into the branches of a tree so that he can keep the enemy under close observation. His men fade away as the sound of galloping hooves tear into the silence of the countryside. The patrol jerks to a halt beneath the tree. Trackers point out the way the men have gone. Orders are shouted and the horsemen wheel their mounts and rush off.

In dismay, Sandawara sees that they are after the main band. Hoping to distract them, he slides down from the tree, drops to one knee, sights and fires. A rider lurches in the saddle, clutching one shoulder. The horsemen scatter. Sandawara ups and lopes away. Behind him the party rallies, one group gallop off while the rest turn and come charging back past the tree.

144

Thudding hooves shake the ground behind the fleeing black man. He dashes through the scrub and brush. For three kilometres he holds the distance between them. Then a bullet springs off a tree trunk next to his head. Another thuds into the earth right at his feet. Two horsemen spur their mounts in a dead run at him. Sandawara flings up his Winchester and lets off a wild shot.

The men yell and keep on coming. Their revolvers bang out harmlessly. The freedom fighter races off, slowly and surely outrunning the tiring animals. The men curse and flog their mounts. It is a mistake. They should pull up for accurate fire. Sandawara charges through the bush, stops and takes a leap to one side. He rolls down into the steeply sloping mouth of a cave.

Meanwhile the hard riding members of the other part of the patrol overtake Ellewara and Captain's group just as they are hurrying up the incline leading to the hills. The police are almost on them when they drop to the ground and open fire. A rider falls and the others rein in. The band leap to their feet and retreat, not up towards the ridge top, but towards a rocky gorge. The horsemen thunder after them, revolvers popping like cap pistols. A few rein in and aim their rifles. A man, Lillewara, running next to Ellewara, gives a scream as a bullet rips into his back and tears its way out of his chest. Ellewara turns towards his stricken comrade. A great thud is followed by a flash of light. A slug has ripped across his skull. Captain reels and falls moaning with a smashed shoulder. He tries to aim his gun, but a slug has smashed his Schneider into uselessness. Stunned more by the loss of his beloved gun than by his wound, he fails to see the wildly galloping constable who, as he passes, swings his rifle butt down on to the wounded man's head.

He regains consciousness to find himself chained to Ellewara. Cold links circle their necks. No one has attended to their wounds. Burning with hate they direct their scornful eyes to the Queensland trackers who speedily wilt under the concentrated venom of the chilling gaze. They see their deaths reflected in the eyes of the freedom fighters and turn away. If Captain and Ellewara should ever escape, the whole of Australia will not be able to hide or guard these traitors from justice.

Ellewara recovers from the scalp wound and his rage is a shield around him. He stands tall and proud, unbowed by the iron around his neck. Has he not been captured before and escaped? No one can steal his freedom from him. His breath is one long hiss of flame and lust for revenge. Without traitors, the invaders would never have captured him. He looks at Captain. Ready, as he is, for the first opportunity to escape.

The horsemen turn and canter off. The chain tightens. The wounded prisoners are forced to lope along behind the animals.

Captain's chill rage turns over the escape methods of the prisoners he has guarded when a slave of the white men. What they have done, he can do better. His hard eyes bore into the uneasy backs of the trackers riding ahead, then he twists his head towards his comrade.

Ellewara rages at his plight. They will never hold him, but they do – until he gains eternal freedom dangling at the end of a rope in Derby Town.

Captain is not from the Kimberleys. Originally, the white men have taken him from South Australia to do their dirty work for them far from his own land, but he has grown to love the crags and fastnesses of the Leopold Ranges, a land very different from his flat dry desert. Now he is leaving it for ever and moving closer to home, but not near enough for his spirit to return there. He is to be exiled on Rottnest Island off the port of Fremantle. There he will suffer with others of his people. Penned like an animal in a concentration camp designed to break men, especially a free man, for a year he will build roads and mine salt under the lash. Shackles will turn his ankles into running sores as he slaves to secure the land for the invaders. Then in a desperate attempt to regain his freedom, he will try to escape by swimming the fifteen kilometres of rough sea separating the island from the mainland. Dragged down by his chains and almost drowned, he will be pulled out and then flogged by his captors. It will take just over a year to break his spirit. He is a tough one, this Captain. Most men break within months.

III

Sandawara scrambles back to the cave mouth and aims his rifle at a rider. He fires. Blam! He frowns. The man's hat zips off his head. He lowers his aim. Blam! Again the shot goes wild. A horse goes down and threshes about. Sandawara examines the sights of his Winchester, while the party gallop out of the line of fire. He pumps a bullet into the breech. Blam! A hundred metres off, a leaf rips off a twig. He smiles and waits.

Bitter despair at the upsetting of his plan hits his heart, then his mood lightens. The main body of his men have made it to the hills and are now resting before marching back to attack the camp. Night falls as he waits to escape. With the police so near who will believe that the freedom fighters would be foolhardy enough to strike out?

Under the sheltering rock, he listens while staring up at the darkening sky. A few grass blades outlined at the cave mouth vanish in the gloom. He takes a quick nap. Sounds jerk him alert. He fires a couple of shots, then relaxes. Time broods on in the cool, deep silence. He becomes detached from the mad outside world where men kill and are forced to kill. If only the strangers followed Wandjina, then they would know and follow the Law. Then no more trouble. But the invaders follow no law he can understand. Are they really human or other than human, he wonders about the invaders who have forced brother to fight brother, who kill each other and seem to hate the very earth.

He crouches unable to understand. He listens to the deeper drip-drip of subterranean water which is the heartbeat of the earth and thinks of himself as a child. The touch of his naked mother as she feeds him from her body, the gleam of the fire at night, the tall hardness of his father. All these have made the security of his life – then the strangers came to bribe him into becoming an enemy of his earth and an outlaw named Eaglehawk. He had forgotten Wandjina for a long time, now no more. He defends Wandjina's people and his Law, but the police rage against him. He forsook his ancestors and broke the Law to ride with the police, now he suffers the fate of all lawbreakers.

He is hunted and driven from place to place. He is tracked like an animal and if caught is to be killed without mercy. Death is his future, he knows it, by a bullet or a rope. He has broken the Law and can never be an elder of his people knowing all the sacred songs and rituals. He hopes the end will be a bullet. Eaglehawk, the tracker, has seen men hanged, their legs kicking at air, their eyes bulging from the sockets, a blackened tongue hanging from a drooling mouth, the neck snapping like the branch of a tree. He grins without mirth, remembering the stiff penis and the last ejaculation. Is the spirit leaving the body to return to the source? The question is left to die. He is a warrior, still young and agile – not an elder – and his duty is to fight, to gain victories, to gather men and train them into an army to expel the aliens from the land. Spiritual matters should be left to those who understand them.

Sandawara stares up at the darkened cave mouth and it seems that a small, black figure stoops and enters. It is his old mother lugging a dilly bag stuffed with good chunks of roo meat, freshly seared in a fire. He is about to greet her when she vanishes. He blinks his eyes. It has been a spirit woman come to comfort him. Sandawara feels fresh and invigorated as if his strong white teeth have ripped into the juicy flesh.

Scuffling noises! Quickly he fires two shots. Briefly he thinks of his men. From a distance, sporadic gunfire is heard. Are they in contact with the enemy? The firing peters out. No, he is sure his men are safe in the hills and regrouping for the dawn attack. More sounds at the cave mouth. He empties his rifle and slowly reloads. He knows his cave. It extends back a hundred metres and tapers to a dead end. Another tunnel branches to the right, but this ends in a pool of water. Only the one entrance, but the warrior is untroubled. In the dead of the night he can slip by them.

Suddenly, without warning, a rock glances off the floor at his feet. He leaps up and races to the back of the cave. A shower of rocks clatter down, bouncing and leaping off the stone walls. The sounds echo and re-echo. Sandawara grins. They'll never drive him out with such tactics. The stones cease and he returns to his old position. The night creeps on, and he prepares to escape.

Just as he is about to make his attempt, the cave mouth glares with light. Sandawara curses. A watchfire has been kindled almost directly in front of the entrance. Now there is no chance of a stealthy upward crawl, the sudden silent leap into the open and into the darkness, then the race away before the police are even aware of his escape. No chance of that now with the fire flinging its light right down to him. Guns are sure to be trained on the cave mouth, ready for the break. Up above, death stands armed and waiting for him while below in the earth, what? Slow, starving death or surrender! Never surrender – only death!

Sandawara creeps perilously close to the open air. So close that the fire glares on his fierce face and on the cicatrised weals and scars on his chest which are the marks of a warrior. A shot. He tumbles down on to the cave floor. Instantly on his feet, he scrambles back to return the fire. Hopelessly trapped, but at least he has a supply of water. He goes to the underground pool and kneels down. His mouth sucks up the water without disturbing the surface, then he returns to his old position. How to escape? His eyes turn blank, unseeing – or seeing? An old man, grey haired and bearded but still sturdy, enters the cave as his mother has before. The elder brushes past Sandawara who watches him disappear into the darkness, then gets up to follow him to the dead end. The ancient one points at the rock face, turns and gazes at the warrior, then vanishes.

Startled, Sandawara stands staring at the stone wall. At last he takes out his knife and jabs it into the rock. It crumbles. The warrior gives thanks to the guardians of his tribe as he hacks into the yielding rock.

Throughout the night he digs and rests, digs and rests. His rest periods are spent sending a bullet or two up at the police – those fools who think him trapped! He laughs as his knife sinks into claylike stone. It is only a matter of clearing out a wedge-shaped fault in the solid rock. The cleft almost seems to grow of its own accord.

Just before dawn Sandawara thrusts in his knife and it passes through into the open. Swiftly he works until the hole is wide enough for him to crawl through, then rushes back to the cave mouth where the fire still blazes. He listens. Not a sound except for the crackling of burning logs. He fires a shot, then runs back to squeeze through the hole and out to freedom.

Sandawara finds himself at the bottom of a cliff right on the edge of a river. Without a splash he slides into the water and floats away as dawn greys the sky. Behind him, the weary watchmen try to stay awake and alert. At last they have trapped the demon, Eaglehawk, like a snake in its hole. But they cannot help thinking of his previous, uncanny escapes. This time they are sure that they have him; but how long will it take to starve him out? They want to end it quickly. They desperately need the glory of catching or killing the most notorious killer in the Kimberleys. Promotion and a transfer south to Perth will take them away from this hated land for ever. The white policemen gloat over their future rewards while the trackers watch the cave mouth. Their reward will be an extra plug of tobacco and a pat on the head. Meanwhile as the policemen's thoughts drift over such subjects, their quarry trots through the growing day, free on his beloved land.

ELEVEN

THE NUNGAR VOTE

Detective Collins, impersonating his favourite T.V. cop, lumbers towards the police car. Unfortunately without the proper camera shots, he makes little impression. Kelly heaves his body after him, like some out of condition rhino. The race is neither won nor lost. The two fall puffing into the back seat of the car, get their breaths and yell to the driver: 'Let's get moving to the Commonwealth Bank! Step on the gas! Just got a hot tip that it's going to be hit by a gang of armed men!'

The over-excited driver screams out of the garage on shrieking wheels. He rockets around a corner and, with his siren ripping into the heat, pelts along for a good two hundred metres. He slams on the brakes, lurching Collins and Kelly suddenly forwards, then abruptly backwards. Apologetically he looks back at them. Behind the car a police van bulging with cops bangs to a halt with a clang of metal on metal. The sedan leaps forward on locked wheels.

'Fuck it, why'd you stop like that?' Kelly shouts out.

'Beg pardon, sir, but which branch of the bank do you want?' Two large meaty faces exchange glances. Steely eyes turn shifty. 'What bank was it, Collins?' Kelly grinds out.

'Thought you caught it,' Collins grinds back, seeing his promotion flying out of the window.

'Get that loony, he can't have got far,' Kelly shouts out, desperately wishing for the services of a good script writer.

The sedan surges off to the end of the street and again slams to a halt. The van bashes into the back.

'Watch it, mate,' the car driver calls over the radio, 'that's the second time you've smacked my arse.'

'Well give some bloody hand signals or something,' the radio squawks back. 'I can't read your bloody mind and your brake lights are on the blink.'

'They bloody well should be after you've smashed them,' the driver snarls as he U-turns and tears back up the street. The van, after a good deal of backing and forwarding, manages to make the turn. It lumbers along with a clashing of gears and a fumbling of clutch.

Meanwhile a good distance ahead in the police car, Kelly and Collins perspire and curse the nut who's causing all the fuss. If the bank is done and they miss it, they'll be up the creek for sure. Things are not too good for the police in the golden west.

Twin cars reflect in Ron's sunglasses as he glances sideways to the kerb. They hurtle past and out of his eyes with a scream of tortured siren – which suddenly falters, gurgles and dies in long drawn out wails. The sedan skids to a halt with a spray of rubber, then reverses with a high pitched whine of protest. Ron pretends to ignore the manoeuvre. The black van cruises to a stop beside him. The man bends over a litter bin and begins to pull out the contents, carefully piling them at his feet.

The crash of the reversing car carooming off the front of the heavy van causes his body to stiffen. He slowly looks up and finds surprise and amazement. The crash ejects a dozen armed cops from the back of the van. They've just been about to leap out in the best possible style when disaster struck. Now they tumble out in a heap of 'fucks', 'hells' and 'it just ain't our day'. Ron looking on has a sudden flash of sanity. There isn't any place for a loony in this world anymore. The competition is too much. He begins carefully replacing the litter. If he doesn't watch out the cops'll be fighting him for food scraps.

The blue heap manages to sort itself out, untangling pistols and batons and handcuffs. They get into some sort of order trying not to show signs of aches and pains from scrapes and bruises. They straighten their uniforms and caps while the wanted man looks down. His shades reflect heavy pig boots that can maim and break bones. His extended flash of sanity becomes terrifying.

'Right, no nonsense, that bank, where is it?!' Collins and Kelly shout. Their words mix into gibberish. The frightened nut seeks refuge in his loony act. He even begins to drool. Inwardly he quakes: 'this game ain't worth a cracker, mate.' Still, he goes into his 'got a twenty cent piece?' routine until the two burly detectives almost throw a fit.

They shake him backwards and forwards and promise him all sorts of hell if he doesn't answer their questions quick-smart. Their hard eyes of steel fuddle his brain.

'You tell us where that bank is or we'll lock you up and throw away the key,' they scream out. 'Where is it? Where is it? Where is it?' they shout over and over again.

The Beaufort Street nut finally recovers enough to begin deciphering the gibberish of their code. He listens, keeping the armour of his lunacy up as a shield. Under it, he is almost in a panic. His heart tears at his throat and breaks the numbness of his life. The flash of sanity has become almost unendurable. 'This game ain't worth a cracker, mate,' he whispers to no one as a coin is thrust into his hand. The detectives have decided to try bribery.

'You know that one in Oxford Street,' he manages to stumble out and is amazed at the result.

The police exit flings him on to the pavement. He sits up in the midst of petrol fumes as motors rev. With a roar first the sedan and then the van charge off with a scream of sirens.

'Dirty pigs,' the man mutters in a shaking voice, slowly getting off the ground. 'Dirty cop bastards, I'll get you for this,' he quakes in a voice which isn't the voice of the Ron of old. He pulls a pair of large, woollen, female underpants from his shirt front and half heartedly flaps them after the vehicles. 'Oh, what's the use?' he almost sobs. His body jack knifes and he heaves up a pound or so of Spam and lumps of bread.

'This game ain't worth a cracker, mate.' He voices the sentence which has been tumbling around and around in his head like clothes in a washing machine. His body is racked by a spasm and jerks green bile down on to the street. He mops his face with the pants, then tosses them into the bin. Instantly his hand leaps out to retrieve them. It stops in mid flight. All at once, the female underpants have turned into just another piece of nondescript cloth. Visions of figures in the mental hospital tumble into his now too sane mind. Frightened, he pushes them down with his newly discovered mantra: 'This game ain't worth a cracker, mate.' The police flock into his head followed by Alan and his mob. He pushes them away. Ron takes the pledge to reform himself – but old habits die hard.

II

'This is it,' Sandawara says with a grin to Kangawara as they wheel along the street. The girl squeezes his hand and prays that everything will go without a hitch. Captain with the bouncing teenybopper on his knee, scowls. Fearing the worst as he does of any situation, he longs only for a drink, and the girl jiggling about means nothing. It's all too crazy for him to make head or tail of. The slogan daubed vehicle stands out a mile, and as for their army fatigues, and as for their stupid masks ... he shudders and shudders again as sirens scream toward them. Ellewara doesn't turn a hair. He keeps on driving steadily, purposely forward. Already he can see his new set of drums. He beats out a rhythmic series of beeps on the horn that makes Captain quake. If only the pigs stop them, if only ... The sirens scream ever nearer.

'What in hell's that?' the driver yells over his radio to the van.

'Looks like some sort of political rally,' Kelly says to Collins.

'Probably university students,' Collins replies to Kelly.

'Want me to pull them over, sir?' the driver enquires helpfully.

'We're on our way to foil a bank holdup and you want to stop a carload of hippy students,' Kelly sneers. 'Man, use that lump you call a head!'

The driver scowls and mutters under his breath.

Ellewara pilots the car sedately along. The police sedan and van scream past. 'Wonder where they're off to in such a rush?' he says to Sandawara.

'They aren't going in our direction, anyway,' the leader replies.

'Maybe they're going to arrest a drunk,' Captain says in an attempt at a joke at which Kangawara smiles.

Next to him Wawollu has her hand down Lillewara's pants and is gently pulling on his pubic hair. This, she knows, quickly turns him on. She wriggles around on his hard penis. Captain doesn't notice just as he doesn't feel the teenybopper wriggling on his lap. Wandara and Terawara are all eyes and pounding hearts and happy to be along for the show. 'Gee, just think, going on a real bank bust just like on telly,' whispers Terawara to her friend. Their cup of happiness overflows. Sandawara and Ellewara will look after them.

Ellewara deftly parks the car outside the bank. He knows that the tyres will be exactly an inch away from the curb edge.

'All right this is it,' growls Sandawara in his deepest voice. His eyes reach out to each person. Everyone is ready for action. His mob get out the rifles and quietly leave the car. In the near- deserted street no one spares a glance for the guerrilla outfit – except the pizza man who stares, then shrugs his shoulders. It's too crazy for him to understand and he's having problems of his own. His wife is just about to have a *bambino*, that is, he wants a son.

Fatalistically he bites into a piece of pizza knowing that the baby'll be a girl. In the distance sirens howl.

The police car hurtles along and at last the driver decides to speak. He's fed up to the gills with his so-called bloody superiors. 'Bloody oafs,' he mutters, then he smirks maliciously, savouring the dropping of his bomb. If only his application to the Commonwealth Police has been accepted, then goodbye to these hicks. He clears his throat.

'Sir,' he begins carefully masking the triumph he is feeling. He hopes they'll be on the mat for this blunder. 'Sir,' he begins again, a joyful edge to his tone. This'll show these bastards up. It'll go down in history. He lets the words out slowly. 'This is a pretty long street and if I recollect rightly there are at least three branches of the bank along it. Which one do I make for?'

'The nearest one, you fool,' scream Kelly and Collins unable to mask their consternation. Their first big job and everyone and everything is letting them down.

'Get on the radio,' yells Collins.

'Get cars to the other branches,' shouts Kelly.

'We want to be at that branch in one minute,' scream the two detectives. 'You're on report,' they scream again when they notice his smirk. Hidden from sight by the front seat they wring their hands. What else could happen?

The sedan rushes back on its tracks. The van carooms around and follows. Two innocent vehicles trying to avoid the police van career out of control and smash head on. No one is hurt, but the police image suffers. The police charge down on the bank and reach it just as Sandawara's mob is rushing out.

'They got guns,' screams Kelly.

'Take no chances,' bellows Collins.

The cops in the van take one long look at the masked and armed robbers and fear hurls them to the ground behind the van for cover. Immediately they sweep the area with concentrated fire.

Ellewara, the wolfman, sitting behind the wheel of the slogan daubed car gapes as the sedan and van screech to a halt and from across the street direct a withering fire at his friends rushing from the bank. Detective Kelly squeezes off three quick shots without aiming and Ellewara stops thinking, for ever, about his drum set. Two of the rounds enter the side of his face ripping his mask, shattering his jaw bone and tearing off plastic and skin.

The third 38 slug passes through his ear to pulp his brain.

Captain, a little ahead of the rest of the mob, tries to lift his rifle. Fatalistically he smiles knowing that he's been right all along. A cop fires twice. Two bullets sock into his belly. Captain falls, blood seeping, then rushing from the wounds below his navel. His lips feel dry and he needs a drink badly. His body is numb, but he knows that he is badly wounded and may be dying. Captain hopes he is. His eyes reach out to Sue, he forgets her new name. 'Hey, man,' he manages to groan. 'Man, I'm hurt bad. Please get me a bottle. Please!' Blackness sweeps Sue away from his sight for ever.

The girl looks for Alan. It's bad for them, but she wants her leader to make it, wants him to be free. She doesn't care about herself, only about the kid she has grown to love as a man. All about her the bullets fly and all she can do is picture Alan standing naked in front of her. Then Captain falls in reality and real fear hits her. It is not in the plan. Alan has been so confident. God, they're firing real bullets at just a bunch of kids. She suddenly feels the weight of her rifle, but can't make the attempt to lift it, let alone aim it at the police.

A cop with a newly issued riot gun lets fly. Sue has taken a step towards Tom. Now a series of hard burning impacts hit her abdomen and chest. The girl is flung up and backward. Blood gushes from the many holes in her body as she crashes to the pavement. A last thought of Alan, no Sandawara, turns her dying eyes in search of him. They can see only the sky. Then a bullet shatters against the side of her mask spraying plastic, bone and grey brain matter around. Her body convulses for a few seconds, then subsides except for random twitches of legs and arms.

The poor teenyboppers have trailed the last out of the bank. Dumbly they huddle against a wall and watch the others cut down. Directly in front of them Rob and Rita (the new names are forgotten) stand exposed to the full blast of the police guns. Cement dust puffs up as bullets skid across the pavement. Whining slugs whip past their ears and prang off the wall. Scared, they huddle together. Their weapons against their bodies and their eyes on Rita raising her rifle and pulling the trigger. Not even a click, the safety catch is still on.

The girl puts herself in front of her lover. A sharp stab of pain as a bullet rips between side and arm searing the skin. She turns to smile encouragement at her man. A slug thuds into her chest and lung. With a grunt of despair, the girl slumps to the footpath. Rob with a scream of agony sprawls over her body to protect it. Bullets rip into his back, between the shoulder blades, further down – at the waist, the hip and the buttocks. Two pass straight through him to wound the girl in the chest. A small trickle of blood from her mouth fills his eyes as his head falls to one side of it. A strange rattling noise comes from his woman. Desperately he tries to lift his head to give her one last kiss, but can't. Rita cannot see her Rob, but can feel for ever the weight of his body as she dies.

The two teenyboppers are the last to go. They are swept away from the wall contemptuously. Discarded, they lie lifelessly, huddled against each other.

The police fire tapers off. 'Got all the bastards,' a jubilant voice shouts.

'Cease fire, men,' Kelly calls getting to his feet from behind the sedan.

Five bodies lie scattered with five rifles in front of the bank. Each rifle's safety catch is firmly on. A cop vomits when he realises that they have shot down a few kids who didn't even know how to use their guns. The newspapers bring out a special edition, headlined: HOODLUMS BATTLE POLICE. Kelly and Collins are the heroes of the day. A few details are suppressed and a few more distorted, but, all in all, it has been a great day for the police.

The result is two new Detective Sergeants, a listless Commonwealth policeman soon to become strangely hooked on dope and six human bodies rotting away, just as their lives would possibly have done. Such is fate for some in the golden west.

TWELVE

DEATH AND BIRTH

His mob have been take from him. Dead or captured. The fiery Ellewara languishes in captivity, his impulsiveness shackled. Captain lies in the jail at Derby, free only in the songs of the people. An evil dry wind scours the land, killing the grass and driving the white-fellow-named 'Eaglehawk' before it. Helpless as a grass seed, he swirls with the wind. Over the dry plains, down through rocky gorges drained of moisture, sipping only a few precious drops of life from hidden soaks. Always on the run, forced on by the patrols riding and searching, seeking out a trace of Eaglehawk. But Sandawara flies above the land leaving never a track. Not a trace of his passing and the traitors are baffled. The trained dogs cast about for scent. The white men smile confidently. Their boys will sniff out the black man who has risen against them with a snarl of defiance on his lips and a rifle in his fist. Now, at long last, they have him on the run and press forwards to finish him off.

Sandawara flees, more a victim of despair than a hunted animal. He feels that his cause is nearly lost. He needs to go to the strong centre of his earth, to regain strength and to feel the powerful wisdom of his ancestors flaming through his veins. Thin and desperate, he is tormented by evil spirits and giant demon dingoes lope after him. His behind is skinny, a skin stretched over a bony framework; his ribs stand out like his manhood scars, and his face is deep-lined with a care turned into dejection. His skin flakes with sweatless mud and ashes. Sandawara slinks, a part of the landscape. The dry grass of his hair and beard, long and matted, sunbleached, squirms in the wind like sand snakes. But even now, the quick lithe movements of his body and the proud poise of his head mark him as Sandawara, the greatest of the freedom fighters. Despairing and alone, a prey to a thousand fears that seem just as real as the men hunting him, he is not about to admit defeat. He needs rest, he needs comrades around him, he needs the strong places of his earth. His eyes, deepset and bloodred, sadden at the memory of his old band. Ellewara, his proud spirit destroyed by a rope. The same with Lillewara. The same with the others. The faithful Captain, his right arm, obeying his every command has gone to the dreaming or to the white man's hell. Sandawara stops fleeing. He stands, then sinks to the ground to rest. Only an instant to shrug off his despair, then he stands again. He is alive and close to the borders of his land. There, no one will be able to find him or get a single word of his whereabouts from his people.

Behind him a column of smoke rises in warning. He pushes his tired legs into a lope. Soon he will be at a place of safety for rest and recovery, then out against the invaders again.

The warrior stops and turns in his tracks. In front of him the smoke puffs up. Sandawara has stopped running like a dog. The setting sun streaks his shadow towards the smoke. An hour and darkness will fall, then he can return, investigate and if necessary, fight!

II

Constable Christian believes that he's tracked Eaglehawk for over thirty miles (rather his tracker, simply called 'Mick' has relied on his instincts and led the patrol towards Sandawara's home territory) and is confident that they'll lay the blighter by his heels the next day. Setting up his camp on the dry bed of Mount North creek, he has supper cooked and after leisurely eating, stands watching the brilliant stars before suddenly becoming conscious of the tall dry grass all around, and going back to the campfire. With a few curt words to the trackers to keep a sharp lookout, he turns in, rolling himself in a blanket even though the weather is warm. With a slight smile on his weathered lips he escapes from the land. Eaglehawk is the prize he is sure of winning and he is out to outdo his partner and gain all the credit. Christian drifts off away from the murmur of the two trackers – to awaken as the tracker, Mick, gently shakes his arm. 'Boss, I hear something, maybe Eaglehawk out there.'

Christian rests on an elbow and hears only the silence of the night. 'Nothing, you fool, get Winega to relieve you. Get some rest, you're hearing things. All you blacks plenty frightened of the dark.'

Winega bears watch to the dawn. He, too, is certain that someone or something is prowling around the camp, but since the big boss doesn't want to be worried, he isn't. Dawn sweeps up pushing the darkness before it. Still the feeling persists that someone has the camp under observation. Winega pokes the fire and puts the billy on to boil. The only sounds are the quiet breathing of the sleeping men, the bubbling of the boiling water and the swish of the evil wind moving the grass. The tracker knows that a blackfellow could move right up to the camp concealed by moving grass. Someone could come right up to, but not away without revealing himself. But the tracker knows that that Sandawara can do anything, can even make the wind turn and move away with him. Winega looks at the bosses sleeping on, separated from each other by the fire and a petty argument. 'Lazy fellows,' Winega tells Mick who has been up since dawn. They drink a mug of tea, then go to bring in the hobbled horses.

With a little trepidation, they pick up the bridles and move into the high grass. The bosses should be up when they return. The white men sleep on. The two trackers follow the marks of the horses' hooves. The sharp crack of a rifle rips the two sleepers awake. They fumble for their revolvers then, wide awake, leap for cover behind the saddles. A pistol bangs and Blythe curses while Christian grins. His partner has accidently shot himself in the hand. Blood spurts out and Blythe wraps his handkerchief around the wound. He knows he will never live it down. Grass moves towards him and he snaps off a couple of shots. Winega falls dead. Blythe curses some more and Christian broadly grins, He has had his revenge and is ready to forgive his partner, though he will spread the story around Derby. A more cautious Mick glides up and says: 'Winega got it through the head, Eaglehawk got me in the arm.' He shows his bloody shoulder and Christian tells him to tear off the tail of his shirt and wrap it around the wound. Another rifle shot cracks out and Christian quickly hugs the ground and prays behind the flimsy protection of the saddles. Mick disappears into the grass where it is much safer.

The two white men blaze away, giving Sandawara the chance to slip off. Finally, they get to their feet. 'Eaglehawk got Winega,' Blythe says, going to the dead black man and turning him over with his boot. 'Yeah,' Christian agrees. 'Now who'll get the bloody horses with him dead and Mick with a wounded shoulder?'

'Arrh Mick isn't hurt that bad. He can help you,' the crestfallen Blythe says, trying to retrieve at least something out of his defeat. For one wild moment he contemplates putting a bullet in Christian's head and claiming Eaglehawk has done it, but the very thought of the news spreading that one man has defeated an entire patrol deters him. He can live down his hand and the shooting of a tracker, but not that.

The horses have not wandered far. They easily find them and saddle up. Christian is happy to have an excuse to turn back. He is happier still when they come up with another patrol. Now for sure they'll run that black snake to his hole, dig him out and break his back. Blythe, Mick and the body of the dead tracker are sent off to the nearest station and Christian joins the patrol. He wants to be in at the kill. They spur their horses on. But Sandawara has found a reservoir of energy and is twenty kilometres away, heading for the headwaters of Mount North creek and the dark tunnel which can take him under and through the mountain range and out into the heart of his country. Behind him the big patrol thunders along without aim or direction. On the off chance that Eaglehawk will stick close to water, they follow in his invisible tracks.

<h1 style="text-align:center">III</h1>

By late afternoon Sandawara is limping. Dogtired and hungry, he moves slowly in the direction of the tunnel mouth. In fifteen or twenty minutes he will be there.

The sound of thudding hooves causes him to whirl around. Groggy and exhausted he has allowed himself to be surprised. The horsemen are almost on him; one of the trackers lets out a triumphant shout. Two men gallop to cut him off, others race directly at him. The dazed warrior stands and stares then, almost too late, leaps onward with his last burst of speed. His will tugs his body away towards safety. He will win through!

He races along the creek bed. No chance and no place to hide. Boulders and soft sand slow the horsemen and give him a chance. He jumps up and over a boulder. One of the trackers stops and lets fly with a shotgun. Sandawara feels the pellets eat into his skin and bones. They serve only to drive him on. On one side a cliff rears. He leaps on to a ledge, then scrambles higher and higher – towards the free open sky. His eyes glaze out into infinite space and figures seem to beckon him on. Behind him the intruders dismount for better aim. Their singing bullets sound like the drone of a bullroarer calling him to a mysterious initiation which the old men have kept hidden from all. The lead smacking off the rocks patters out the clap sticks of the sacred dance. The sacred joy of the corroboree swirls all space about him. A thud at his thigh marks the first cut of the initiation rite. The pain of the bullet is the sharp cut of the flint knife. He wins through, is up and over and flat on his belly on the cliff edge.

The warrior watches, as if from another world, as the pursuers begin scaling the rock face. He aims his rifle and fires twice, then reaches for his cartridge belt to reload. It has gone. It has been pulled off on the climb.

Sandawara cannot hold them off, but in his detached state it does not matter. Phantom hands reach down and pull him to his feet. Some liquid seems to pass his lips and then the soft meat of his forbidden totem animal. His thigh is stiff and runs with blood, but that is as it should be. He allows himself to be drawn away. They are taking him to a safe place. Blood splashes follow him to a deep, dark cave. He enters into the land of his ancestors. He sees the skull-like faces burning down on him. He lies in the depth of his earth, secure in the knowledge that he has come home. Outside the police patrol shouts and circles warily around the cave mouth. He has no bullets, but is unafraid in this sacred place. They cannot enter. He smiles.

At last he must move on again. He is not to die in this cave. He has strength, though the blood is spurting from his thigh – but that is as it should be. Sandawara must move on and keep secret this sacred dreaming place of his people. He turns his back on the cave entrance and begins crawling into the depths. Another way out has been shown to him. His hands and feet mate with the floor and it flows onwards and upwards. Behind, his blood marks the earth in homage, in love and the living rock sups upon it. He is to be reborn. The earth pushes him upwards to the clear light of the sky.

Again he has outwitted them. Never will they catch him, take him away from his earth to the white man's prison, to the white man's rope. Sandawara may die but, if he is to die, it will be in his land and free under his sky. His death will be that of a fully initiated warrior, proud and liberated. Ahead the exit twinkles with tiny stars: the campfires of his ancestors. He rests, listening and letting the night wind beckon him on. He receives the invitation to join them and moves on. Nearer and nearer he approaches the fires of his ancestors. His blood dries and his wound stops throbbing. He gets to his feet, using the rifle as a crutch and hobbles out into the open air. A warrior walks straight and upright, not squirming on his belly along the ground. So it was in the beginning, so it is in the end. He moves out and away across a wide plateau. He picks up a stick and it helps him to limp on. The land wraps him around and eases him along ...

Dawn breaks over the huddled camp of his pursuers. In daylight they gain confidence, but no one enters the cave after Sandawara. The trackers know that it is sacred and are scared for their lives. The white men are afraid to venture into the gloom after the warrior. They order the trackers to cast about for an exit. The sun leaps up and over the mountains. The light glints a golden red off the blood splashes, still fresh and shiny-wet along the rocky ground. Sandawara is bleeding again. A shout and the pack is in full pursuit.

Minutes pass and then far ahead they see the hobbling Sandawara marching towards the sun. His long shadow reaches back to mock them, to menace them. They slow, but creep closer and closer – to the man who is not even aware that he is being followed. The trackers shudder as the warrior stops and turns towards them. Upright and proud, he stands there. A smile lights his face, then he sinks to the earth. The pack seeks cover and opens fire. Bullets lash toward the man, but there is no sound or movement from him.

At last the trackers gingerly approach the fallen figure and circle it. They edge in and stand looking down. The white men are far off. The black men stare at their fallen brother and watch as he stirs and gets into a sitting position. 'Brothers, the white man can never take what I have,' he gently murmurs, then falls back into freedom.

IV

Sandawara ducks back into the bank, his eyes shuddering with the vision of his mob being wiped out. The rattle of gunfire sounds and resounds in his ears. The terrified bank employees, still huddled on the floor, stare blankeyed at him. Quickly he snatches up a thick wad of banknotes, spilled from Wawollu's sack, then rushes to the back of the building. The bolted door is as Kangawara described it. He tears it open and charges through and out. Behind him the guns stutter into silence. He flees out of the backyard and into the alley. His mind is filled with the falling bodies of his comrades. All dead, wounded or captured, and tears fill his eyes, overflow and wash away his childhood. They are his warrior scars and are as deep and as permanent. Behind him he leaves his childhood days. Ellewara, Kangawara, Captain, the two teenyboppers, wide-eyed and dead in innocence. He rips off his animal mask, flings his useless rifle up on to a low roof and takes off the overalls. He must get out of the city – to the bush. He longs for the bush, for the country far from roads and the sight of white faces. He tucks the wad of money into his pocket. It will take him far from the city hell.

'Hey mate, got twenty cents for a cup of coffee?'

Sandawara blinks up into the face of Ron. The man straightens up from a rubbish bin, stuffing a white petticoat under his shirt. The youth tries to give one of his carefree grins, but cannot. Instead his face appears to crinkle up in pain.

'Sounded like shots back there. Know what happened?'

'Don't know, didn't go out of my way to see. Got to get moving, here.' He thrusts a banknote into the man's hands.

'Gee, thanks, see you at the pad tonight, huh?'

'Maybe, maybe – got to rush off now,' the youth replies and runs off.

Ron's mirror sunglasses reflect the youth's back. Somehow, he's always liked the kid, even though he is a boong. The man looks down at the note, ten dollars, and happily grins. The grin holds for a moment, then collapses. Absentmindedly, the man pulls out the petticoat and drops it on to the ground. Already, he's forgotten his snitching to the police; but a sadness falls into an empty place in his body. Something, he feels, has happened, something terrible like the last few pages of a good story flickering to a tragic end and the sudden awareness of the reader that soon he will be alone again. Ron knows the crashpad is over, that he will never go there again because it will not be there to go to. Slowly he bends, picks up the petticoat and drops it back into the litter bin. The sunglasses follow. His pale blue eyes soak up the sun. He finds himself perspiring and takes off his coat. He blinks as he opens his shirt to the air. All at once he thinks about getting a job. Too many things have happened that he cannot remember, but they were deadly things. He shakes his head. Too many things rattling around inside. Time for a change, the man thinks as he moves out on to the street without his armour ...

Noorak sits slumped beside his smouldering fire. An old man lost in the reality of his dreaming, he sees more than others. He has followed

Sandawara to his end and beyond. As a boy of nine he saw the warrior. He stood an arm's length away and watched with saucer eyes as the man, tall and straight, talked to the people. He remembers the rifle clutched in the warrior's hand, but he cannot recall what he was saying. He must have spoken about the white men and the boy knew only of white men as some sort of evil spirits. He had not yet seen one in the flesh.

Suddenly loud noises begin and strange singing sounds whizz through the camp. The people immediately make a dash for some nearby caves – all except Sandawara and his band and the terrified little boy, huddled into a fold in the ground, crying for his mother. The warrior points his rifle and it begins booming. The boy stops his crying and stares in amazement at this new world of smoke spitting sticks which go bang. Then he gasps as something hits Sandawara in the head and makes it bleed. Something comes whining toward him and hits the ground beside him. The boy digs it up. His hand closes over a warm little stone unlike any he has seen. Then something gives his leg a sharp blow. The world goes numb and dark. He comes to, whimpering with the pain of the flesh wound, but secure in a strong black arm and with the familiar odour of his people around him. He is carried into a cave, then out into sunshine. The noises seem a long way off. The man puts him down on the warm earth.

'It hurts little fellow, it hurts as much as my head does,' and Sandawara takes the boy's hand and puts it against his head wound. The blood makes the boy's fingers all sticky. Next the warrior touches Noorak's wound and says: 'Never forget that the white men have done this to you. This is your first manhood scar and is to be borne with honour. This'll fix it in no time,' and Sandawara pats fresh ash on to the wounds. 'This'll make you better. You'll get so strong you'll join me in the war against the white intruders.'

The warrior makes the boy feel strange and he begins to whimper. Sandawara consoles him as he would his son: 'Don't worry little fellow, everything's all right.' Then he takes the boy and wedges him in a cleft in the rock. 'Your mum'll be along bye and bye to get you,' the man comforts him, running his rough fighter's hand over his head. The guerrilla band moves off and the boy is left alone, clutching the bullet which has wounded Sandawara. That night his mummy comes, as Sandawara has said, and gets him.

Noorak fingers the ancient leg scar, his first manhood welt. He thinks about the bullet which wounded Sandawara. He kept it for a long time and eventually hid it with other sacred things in his land. The old man stares down into the fire and thinks about the death of Sandawara who died that all men should be free. He thinks of his own life: old Jacky Jacky taken far from his country to languish in a white man's prison, then ejected, old and broken, to live as best he could, bereft of land, hope and people. Far south, too far south and too broken in spirit to attempt the long trek back – until now since a boy has come asking him about the old days and the old ways, asking him about Sandawara and listening as he speaks of the warrior. His old voice murmurs: 'Sandawara, Sandawara,' and it is like a prayer.

'Yes,' Alan, the new Sandawara replies, stepping up to the fire and staring down with the sad eyes of the old Sandawara. His tears have flowed and have dried to sadness. Again he looks just another Nungar youth – except for his eyes. Hard and alert and sad. They soften a little as he says to the old man: 'Granddad, granddad, I have money, let's away up north to your land. Come with me, now!'

'I'm ready,' the old man replies. 'Ready to begin my last journey back to the strong places of my ancestors and to the land which Sandawara called his own. I want to feel again the gullies and hills, the plains and valleys. I want to hear the sound of my own language and help in the old ceremonies. I want to die with my people and in my land with the ancestors.'

Noorak is helped to his feet by the youth. Sandawara carefully puts out the fire. 'That one's been alight for many a year,' the old man says. 'Now no more use.' Strength flows into his bones at the thought of returning to his land. Already he can feel its warmth, the coolness of the breezes blowing there, and the sounds of the sacred dances keeping the land in good repair. He leans on Sandawara and they slowly move away from the bridge and on to the road. In true Nungar fashion the youth has a taxi waiting to take them to the airport. His sense of style has not deserted him. It remains beyond the death of his comrades and the loss of his youth. Now he is a man and he is escorting an elder home. He grins as the taxi moves off. Already he is seeing the worn purples and reds of Noorak's home and Sandawara's land. Noorak is smiling too. Already he feels as good as on his land and with his people. It is long past time for the boy to be initiated into manhood and he will do it as soon as possible.

www.ingramcontent.com/pod-product-compliance
Lightning Source LLC
Chambersburg PA
CBHW031202260626
47169CB00004B/1215